Christopher Homm

D1394426

Christopher Homm

C. H. SISSON

*pristina stabilitas hactenus accipienda est,
quatenus aegritudinem ita nullam corpora
illa patientur, sicut nec ista pati possent
ante peccatum.*

St. Augustine, *Retractationum Liber* I, XI

CARCANET

First published in 1965
© *C.H. Sisson,* 1965, 1975, 1984
First published by Carcanet Press Limited in 1975;
in paperback format in 1984
208-212 Corn Exchange Buildings
Manchester M4 3BQ

Sisson, C.H.
 Christopher Homm.
 I. Title
 823'.914 [F]   PR6037.178
 ISBN 0 85635-567-4

*The publisher acknowledges the financial assistance of
the Arts Council of Great Britain.*

Printed in England by SRP Ltd, Exeter.

Now I am forty I must lick my bruises
What has been suffered cannot be repaired
I have chosen what whoever grows up chooses
A sickening garbage that could not be shared.

My errors have been written in my senses
The body is a record of the mind
My touch is crusted with my past defences
Because my wit was dull my eye grows blind.

There is no credit in a long defection
And defect and defection are the same
I have no person fit for resurrection
Destroy then rather my half-eaten frame.

But that you will not do, for that were pardon
The bodies that you pardon you replace
And that you keep for those whom you will harden
To suffer in the hard rule of your Grace.

Christians on earth may have their bodies mended
By premonition of a heavenly state
But I, by grosser flesh from Grace defended
Can never see, never communicate.

I

HE WAS A PATTERN OF AMIABILITY WHEN HE FELL flat on the gravel. The drop on his nose rolled off and became a ball of dust, but he did not move again and his subsequent history was only a funeral. Enough winters had grizzled his head for the doctor to find natural causes for the ending of that capitation fee. Christopher Homm had not even the parting scandal of an inquest.

He was a prince who had not been much celebrated. The palace in the yard of which he died was 92 Torrington Street, the two hundred and fourteen houses of which were constructed of yellow brick of an unweatherable surface. They were arranged in such form that the house agent, who never had occasion to sell them except in lots of five or six, was able to describe them as terraces on the simple ground that there were no interstices between them. Certain of the houses were distinguished by a television aerial, others by brass pots within which were cultivated plants of great splendour, but in every house there was a different form of corruption.

The corruption of Christopher Homm, when he fell down, became simply physical, but it had been preceded by seventy years of imperfect morality. The failures of the spirit that had inhabited him were visible in that face when the neighbours turned it up. If the flesh were only forgettable dirt one would not grieve for it, but it is a model of what must appear at the resurrection.

The almost white hair lay loosely across the pate of Christopher Homm. When it fell sideways it showed that the pate was bald. A first deception. And then the baldness had no smoothness. This prince was not turned to marble before his time. The dry skin was scrofulous and it was stained. The whole head was inedible.

The eyebrows were more like unwholesome mosses than animal growths. The eyes had been pale, wandering and bloodshot. The wrinkles that formed the despairing sneer had had no juice in them for years. The breath had been sour since adolescence and the lips had no more shape than a bit of an intestine.

A scraggy sleeve of tendons joined the head to its body. The body had shape where there were bones but the skin was more than needed. The body hairs had something of colour and glint still, and the parts that had been the manhood of Christopher Homm looked no more crinkled than the rest of him. The legs were mainly notable for their knees and their varicosities, but his toes were big and twisted enough for remark.

More than half of these shames were hidden by Christopher Homm's blue striped shirt, without collar, and by the trousers of his best suit of hard-wearing grey. It was a pity he was not wearing the whole suit, for in it he was called a respectable old man and went to chapel.

The tin-roofed edifice on the corner of Torrington Street had been the locus of Homm's most considerable orisons. Here he would stand, as often on a Sunday as they would let him, with his grimy eyelids closed, misleading the scruffy congregation in prayer. The sect he belonged to was very democratic. Its deity, maybe, was very ill-informed or at least had, like many of his subjects, a passion for listening to the news. However it might be, Christopher Homm would recite in his prayers statistics of crime and other employment. If the murder rate went up, or men were thrown out of work, the chapel god was sure to hear of it through the lips of Christopher Homm. Homm was not known to pray except in public, but the heart is, of course, unsearchable.

Besides praying, Christopher Homm had as an occupation shopping. In the morning of each week-day he set out with an enormous basket, fastened the door of number 92 behind him, and shuffled to the newsagent's shop at the corner. Here he read the advertisements which, printed in illiterate hands, were displayed in a case affixed beside the hanging carcases of newspapers. The advertisements were of iron bed-steads for sale, three castors missing; good home wanted for working man, non-smoker; attractive model, age nineteen, will take a few engagements, figure or lingerie; woman wanted to do rough work. Christopher Homm had a bed; he did not want to offer a home even to a non-smoker; he had in his day seen lingerie and even figure; and he did his own rough work and did not want a woman about the place. None the less these marvels, inscribed on cards occasionally renewed but always soiled, held him daily for eight or nine minutes. Then he bought the newspaper from which he collected the information which was to be transmitted to his deity at the week-end. He folded the paper and put it into his basket. Then he shuffled to the butcher's where he stared through the window at blood and sawdust until the butcher sharpened his long knife and waved it at him. When this happened he moved on to the grocer. Here he generally bought nothing but he liked to stand for a while among the housewives, pressed if possible against the bulges of the more mountainous. His pretext was that he was looking to see whether there were any arrow-root biscuits.

When Christopher Homm reached home again he took his newspaper out of the basket and put on his spectacles. Then he sat down at the kitchen table, opened the newspaper, and read first of all the advertisements which related to the cure of constipation, the care of the complexion, and the founding of the female figure. When he had done this he turned to the headlines which, being a man of reason above all, he often could not comprehend. He stared at them until the words danced. Then VISHINSKY SLASHES PEACE BID EFFORT became VISHINSKY SLASHES BED EFFORT or the words assumed some other order as meaningful and more interesting than the original. Next came the minor headings. "Police seize cosh hoard: boys charged" and "I won't, says star to £50,000 offer." It was only after long reflection of the newsprint in the pupils of his eyes that anything changed inside the head of Christopher Homm. When a little explosion at last took place it was followed by an interval of darkness.

After a little while the sour humours collecting in his belly caused him to lay aside his spectacles and, straightening his legs with difficulty, to stand up and move towards the w.c. This little act of resolution was a matter of pleasure, for this was the only matter which, on weekdays, ever demanded his presence at a certain time in a certain place. And nothing he did on any day of the week gave him so precise a sense of fulfilled purpose. He had to open the back door, step carefully on to a square of uneven brick, and pull open the cheap board door to his right. The door jammed and, when it opened, quivered and rang like a wooden bell. Once inside, Christopher Homm shut himself in. The light fell only from an opening at the top of the door where one board was sawn off short, and from a small and grimy window to one side. As Christopher Homm sat down the sill of the window was near his eye. He could see the thick dust and grit on it, the refuges of spiders in each corner and the nets they had flung between him and the light. The empty body of a fly vibrated on a web as a draught shook it, and in the corners the legs of the spiders appeared like the whiskers of prawns under a rock. This place was watchful for the chance of a death.

If the weather was not too cold Christopher Homm would here resume his outstaring of newsprint. The news here was a fortnight or a month old, was cut up into oblongs and fastened by a string at one corner. To the ambiguities of the full headline was added the fascination of the odd word and the bisected paragraph. These leaves were sybilline. To Homm they meant more than the complete paper. In this exercise his mind became comparatively lively.

> "*The half-clothed body* . . .
> *woman believed to be that* . . .
> *who, on the previous* . . .
> *police arrested a* . . ."

was evocative as no complete story could have been. Moreover,

> ". . . *Eden*
> . . . *insky*
> . . . *guard*"

called down an angelic host whose arrival had not in fact been reported. If at this moment the sun spilt over the bright edging of the customary cloud, the Lord himself might enter through the gap at the top of the door.

But such visions were not customary. Ordinarily animal reliefs had to be enough. For these alone there was gratitude in the heart of Christopher Homm. And for celebration, when he got back to the kitchen, he would put the kettle on the rusting gas-stove. Then he would take down the tea-pot from the window-ledge. It was a shining orb of a burnt sienna or almost black brilliance. It reflected a depth far greater than its own diameter. The world in it was polished, wicked and uncertain. The nose of Christopher Homm himself was pulled into the depths like a balloon skin being wilfully stretched. The windows buckled and once, oh horror! the baker looked in at the same moment. It was only in recoiling from the face in the tea-pot that Homm turned and found himself looking at a real one. That real face split itself with a roar and showed a gulf edged by white teeth. It was the door of Jonah.

"Small one, dad?"

The baker was gone and Homm was looking at a brilliant sky.

When he made his tea the pot ceased to be magical. It stood burning and still on the kitchen table, but as soon as it had wept into the thick white cup it was snuffed under a cosy. The mind of Christopher Homm then became not eye but palate. Smell was no part of it; that had long since gone in the developing etiolation. But the scalding wetness pouring over the gums and tongue could make the mouth a cavern he was aware of. The lower teeth were like stalagmites with water rustling over them, and it was into a gulf such as swallows a subterranean river that the liquid finally disappeared.

When the tea was gone there came a moment of uneasiness, for swallowing it had mitigated Homm's stupor and promoted a consciousness for which he had little use. He could only resolve to get on with his sorting out. This was the last vice he developed. It was an enfeebled attempt to impose on the world the disorder of his own dissolution. The scene laid for it was the front bedroom, which was not otherwise used. Slowly Homm climbed the linoleum-covered stairs and entered this arcadia. The curtains were always drawn and a green light fell through them. On the floor, on the soiled bed, were tumbled heaps of pillows, letters, old hats, yellow newspapers, bed-clothes. From the heaps peeped out corsets, nightdresses, skirts. Christopher Homm looked with particular blankness at these relics of his departed saint. He knelt on the floor in the midst of all this disorder like a young girl offering herself to the tide. Sometimes he picked up a garment or a letter and let it fall through the fingers of his outstretched arm. Once he fell wildly forward and fought the confusion recklessly, calling out in a dry voice – he thought he was shouting –

"Freedom! Freedom!"

He could not smell the must that his efforts had stirred. He rose, and going from room to room collected old trinkets, a saucepan, an anti-macassar and an armful of disused fire-irons and threw them on to the heap with a glowing heart. It was a last imitation of generosity.

Such was the senile life of Christopher Homm.

II

WHEN FELICIA WAS ALIVE THINGS HAD BEEN DIF-
ferent. The sameness had begun when she died, and the
funeral had been the last event in Christopher Homm's life
which took place in a full context of time. After that there
had been only occasional points standing up out of a dim
sea: the hour of attendance at the tin chapel, the moment of
visiting the w.c.

The funeral of Felicia Homm was a great public event, the
focus of many synchronizations. When the resplendent hearse
started to move down Torrington Street, a feat which had
seem to Homm impossible received public acclamation. The
confusion and worries that had torn the mind of the be-
reaved husband were annulled by the indubitable order of
the procession. Two cars, mournful and reluctant, followed
the hearse. In the first of these sat Homm, looking straight
ahead. He did not wish to look at the street, for neighbours
might have thought that the distraction of pride. Nor did
he want to look to his left, where sat a vast shape disturb-
ingly like the one he knew was lying in the coffin ahead
of him. This was Felicia's sister Sophie who bore, under a
shiny black dress, enormous dependencies of breast and belly
which were contained only by the most determined swad-
dling. The face of Sophie was set in a resolve which was of
the flesh rather than of any disengaged will. The mouth
might have had sub-cutaneous bars parallel with it, concealed behind over- and under-lip, but it was itself without
resolution or intelligence. It was a blind aperture for food,
turned by a trick into a vent for the emission of language.
Whatever mechanism directed that language must have been

situated well below the level of the eyes, for through those windows one looked only on a fathomable blankness. Down each of Sophie's cheeks rolled a tear, for the body said this was grief, and there was a lace-edged handkerchief for the purchase of which grief could have been the only excuse.

The hearse stopped outside the chapel and Felicia's coffin was carried in while the mourners followed less commodiously. Sophie found the steep path difficult, as Felicia would have done if she had not today been going like a lady. Black-tied, dark-clad men with bent spines and drooping moustaches got out of the second car. They would obviously never have succeeded in effecting an entry into the chapel at all but for their anxiety to be in at the derision of a sister whose apparently undaunted flesh had after all failed before their own. Christopher Homm, looking round, could not understand why he had paid for so many free rides. He felt none the less that it was to his credit.

When he and Sophie entered the chapel the harmonium was playing. Its thin whirr gave the impression that they were being sucked in by a vacuum cleaner. The mourners took their places in the pews and prayed by staring at the artificial graining. Then the pastor spoke the many words which he introduced by calling a few.

Our dear sister, that was the gist of what he said, was a valiant soldier of Christ. Those sightless eyes had seen a vision. Some might think it merely the glint of corrugated iron but the pastor knew it to be the shining appearance of the Supreme Man. It was the Supreme Man who had started Felicia behaving in the way she did. The pastor instanced, somewhat inconsequentially, the tea she had served to the Bright Hour. He knew almost everything that had passed in Felicia's heart. He was very well informed too about the Supreme Man, who was so much a man that he was supreme only in the sense that his moral stature was an inch or two above even the pastor's. How did it come about that His appearance had shone? The pastor's hardly did yet, as the matter was laid before the congregation, the pastor and the Supreme Man were kaleidoscopically confused. The two seemed to be neck and neck in the race for heaven. It would have been difficult for even an attentive hearer to decide, as the discourse proceeded, which of the two was winning points for patting kiddies on the head, taking a stand against drink, or denouncing the shame of our great cities. The pastor had difficulty in bringing the harangue back to the subject of Felicia, but he did so at last by suggesting that the personal safe-conduct to salvation he could offer was unanswerably evidenced by the contents of the coffin before him.

The vacuum-cleaner started its music again and the congregation wailed a hymn:

> "*O Lord, O Lord, what wilt Thou say*
> *When Thou look'st down on us today?*
> *'Of these that I so long have fed*
> *Another sinner now is dead.'*"

When that was over, the chairmen carried the Lady Felicia out and the mourners followed saying to one another that it had been a very encouraging address.

The mourners looked encouraged as they stepped into their motor-cars again. They were like the representatives of a very important enterprise, the value of whose shares draped itself about them like a mantle. At the graveside the value of the shares fell. It had been possible for aged men to triumph over the pre-decease of Felicia as she lay in her pomp at the end of the chapel; it was impossible not to share in her abasement as she was lowered into the pit. The very clay that bespattered the shiny black shoes of the mourners seemed to be a paste made of decay that was theirs as well as hers. No words spoken at the graveside managed to displace this preoccupation except in Christopher Homm himself who, at a certain formula, saw Felicia float out of the pit and identify herself with the figure of Sophie standing beside it.

It was as he left the cemetery which had become the home of so many buried felicities that Christopher Homm realized what would be the lack of his own. The hilly acres of white tombstones looked like a battle-field, and the funeral party were defeated survivors. Such remnants of public splendour as had survived the interment disappeared as the formal party was dissipated. For the last time in his life Christopher Homm was set down at his doorstep by mechanized conveyance.

He was then alone. He walked into the front room and looked at his sad figure in the mirror. He had not the appearance of one embarking on a gay widowerhood. The pouches under his eyes were of no temporary grief; they were the marks of the already established defection of his own animal spirits. He ran his finger over the top of the sideboard and left a mark. Already the sideboard needed dusting, but it seemed to Homm physically impossible that it should ever be dusted again.

This sad house had been the scene of Felicia's last agonies. She had laid her great heap of flesh on the bed only a week before she died. It had been a solemnity, with something of finality about it even at the time. Felicia did not make a habit of being ill. She rolled herself out of bed at seven every morning and did not return to it until half-past ten at night. Between those times she worked or perambulated almost without intermission, to her own glory and the shame of a husband who would not do half as much. But one day the will to be in motion suddenly ceased. Felicia did not look ill. It was merely that her eyes ceased to bulge and roll and instead became stony. She went to bed at four in the afternoon. She did not say first that she had a headache, or that she must sit down and see what a cup of tea would do for her. She simply went upstairs and undressed as carefully as usual and did her hair up as for the night. Her husband discovered what had happened only when, at a quarter to five, he found her in bed, lying on her back and staring at the ceiling. He was looking for her because he wanted to ask when his tea would be ready. He did not ask. Felicia's look told him he would get his own. So he made the best of a bad job and offered to get some for his wife. She neither thanked him nor refused. She was simply not interested. When he brought a cup and set it beside her she said in a flat voice that she didn't want it. He asked her if she wanted anything else. She did not. Not even a hot bottle? She had said nothing. When he came back again in three hours she stayed on her back and shouted as if at someone who had worried her incessantly:

"I said I wanted nothing."

Christopher Homm went away. When his bedtime came he entered the room again and undressed without a word. Then in a gingerly fashion he lifted the bedclothes and got in beside his wife. He suspected that her flesh was made of some new material. It did not budge except to register a shallow breathing. He tried to settle at ease beside it, leaving a protective gap at all points between his own body and hers. As he went towards the frontiers of sleep the gap seemed to widen. It became a chasm. He feared it and that prevented him from actually passing into sleep. While, in his dreaming but sleepless condition, he was conscious of the distance which separated his wife's body from his own, he was at the same time tented by an image of her body grown hollow and papery. Within this vast shell he dared not stir until at last terror seized him and without reflection he flung his right hand free of the bedclothes. The image disappeared. He saw only the ceiling, the top of the wardrobe and a bit of its mirror. At his side the real body was still sleeping. He prodded it, but even the breathing ignored him. In a sweat he arose and went downstairs to make himself a cup of tea. As he drank it a resolution formed itself. He would lie alone. He took a rug and stretched himself out on a bed in the spare room. There was luxury about the action. The roughness of the wool on his cheeks evoked the liberty and isolation of his military life, when he had moved within an order of limited obligations. For the moment he was rescued from that descent into bottomless anxieties which his wife's sickness portended. He slept the sleep of a coward released from danger.

It was late and light when he awoke, and he got up at once and crept guiltily into his wife's bedroom as if he came from some frightful indulgence. Felicia was on her back, her eyes were open; she was staring at the ceiling. All that she would say was that she did not want anything. She had not missed him. She did not mind.

Christopher Homm felt that he should lever her out of bed to try whether, once on the floor, she would be capable of movement. As he dared not undertake this enterprise, he decided to see whether the doctor would come. It was a big step to take without Felicia's concurrence. He wondered that he should dream of doing it without her command. Uncertain what to do, he crept to the bottom of the stairs and called out in a whisper that he knew she could not hear:

"Felicia, shall I ask the doctor to come? You ought to see a doctor. I think I'd better go and telephone."

It was not a communication but a confession. After that he was free to go. He closed the door softly and walked to the little post office at the corner of the street. It was a roomful of dull light with a disproportionately large cage across the counter and, along the wall, three cubby-holes separated by vast antique partitions to secure that whatever telegrams or cards were written in them could be written in unsurpriseable secrecy. Christopher Homm went to the obscure telephone box at one end of the counter and fumblingly put on the light. Then he had to put on his spectacles and search for the doctor's name in the directory. At last it was found. The doctor's receptionist consented to record the address only after questioning Homm narrowly as to whether his wife was not well enough to come to the surgery. The receptionist would not say when the doctor would come, but she assured Homm that his name would go on the list and warned him not to ring again. When Homm put down the receiver he felt that he had been excused for his temerity, but barely.

Homm then had to consider whether he should tell Felicia what he had done. He imagined that her previous unnatural apathy might turn into an active ferocity of all her bulk. On the other hand, if he did not tell her, she might when the doctor came stand at the top of the stairs in her nightdress and defy him to come up. Then Homm, cringing in the passage, would have to give an explanation to the doctor. He resolved to speak to her. Standing by the bedroom door he said:

"The doctor might come and see you."

Felicia said nothing and Christopher, not even certain that she had heard him, at length went away, and downstairs considered in the dark front room the appalling events he was in the middle of.

When the doctor came Felicia was pleased to see him. She sat up at once, having already got out of bed to comb her hair and wash and powder herself. She smiled like an important and unfortunate victim. The doctor took her temperature, which was normal, carried out a formal exercise in stethoscopy, and put on a smile of the sort that was common in clergymen when the ignorant sought comfort in that quarter. There was nothing much wrong with her, the doctor said, then, seeing that this disappointed her, added that she must look after herself. He would give her a tonic, he said, getting up from the bed-side and flicking the stethoscope so that it disappeared from view. He smiled again, but became peevish when he saw that he had to do with a patient without faith.

"All right, Mrs Homm," he said menacingly, as he wrote out the prescription. "Take it three times a day after meals." It was as if he had added: "And it will be the worse for you." He added to his prescription what might have been something to make the medicine taste nasty.

Felicia said complainingly that she was not taking any meals, didn't feel she could. The doctor took the line that she ought to do so. If she didn't, it was stupidity, which he did not regard as a disease. He retreated.

"I'll look in again in a week," he said. When he called it was to certify death.

The death of Felicia Homm was merely an accentuation of the apathy that had been her illness. Christopher came in one morning to find her staring at the ceiling harder than ever. He had given up touching her, and he did not try whether she was cold. Instead, he walked round the bed, looking at her first from this side and then from that. He spoke, but he knew that if one spoke even to a live person there need not be a reply. Finally he put his face very near hers, till he was sure that there was no breathing and that her eyes were glassy. He smiled, not that he was glad that she was dead but because of the success of his constatation.

He went out and sat on the top stair. His face began to twitch and finally settle into glumness. Some time later his heart began to feel at any rate the grief of anxiety. How would he ever dispose of that great treasure? The extended body hidden from him by the bedroom door seemed stiff and gigantic. He could not imagine it being carried down the narrow stairs. It might be tipped out of the window like an idol being thrown down. He thought of himself living with it in that upper room for ever.

At last he went out and telephoned the doctor's receptionist who thought, this time, that he had something worth reporting.

III

CHRISTOPHER HOMM HAD LEARNED FROM FELICIA
the shopping which comforted his senility. As practised by
that mistress, the art had, however, an elaboration which it
afterwards lost. To some extent this was inevitable. In
Felicia's hands the game was for two players, or rather for
one player and a worker. Had it been the worker who died
first, however, it is hardly likely that the player would have
submitted to the simplifications which satisfied Christopher
at the end of his days.

Felicia's methods were full of complexities. The preliminary discussion about the day's shopping did not start until
breakfast was over. While Christopher was carrying things to
the sink Felicia, who was meanwhile engaged on more important though less immediately fruitful tasks, began to
harry him. As she was looking into a cupboard she would
suddenly turn her head and say menacingly:

"I shall want one or two things from the grocer."

Then she would circulate until she was half inside the
cupboard at the other side of the kitchen. Again with her
back turned, but with a slow quarter-rotation of the head
like that of a gun being trained on a target, she would
say:

"No, I think I can manage one more day without the
cocoa."

Although Felicia looked round she was not looking at
Christopher. Any point near him was good enough for her
eyes, so long as her mouth sent its words in the right direction. When she had spoken she returned to the cupboard as
if to a secret. Christopher Homm would begin to wash up.

At the first clink of crockery his wife spoke again, this time without turning her head but in a terrible voice:

"Mind those cups!"

Christopher Homm gave the tap a further turn in the hope that the noise of the water would deaden the rattle of the cups. But the ruse was met with contempt:

"You're wasting water!"

This was merely to pull Christopher up short and to give Felicia time to disengage herself from the cupboard and collect her indignation. The real accusation came when her great frontage stood opposite his drooping spine:

"You're splashing water all over my kitchen! You don't care how often I have to go over that floor! All you think of is getting at that paper!"

Felicia always refused to open a paper until evening, "when all the work was done," and it was Christopher's weakness to try to shirk proper employment by reading it in the day-time. This propensity was the subject of grave and frequent charges. Moreover, it played a part in Felicia's shopping game. Christopher Homm did not want to go shopping, but he wanted his paper, which he collected in the course of the same excursion. To keep him unhappy, Felicia had therefore to nag him enough to deprive him of any pleasure he might have at the thought of the paper. If this was not possible, and he showed signs of still looking forward to it, she had to lay on him some additional burden in the form of a complication of what was wanted from the shops. Moreover, although she would naturally wish to drive him out on an expedition so long that it would be disagreeable, if she saw he was looking forward to the paper she often elected, at the last moment, to hold him back while she revised her shopping order. It was a source of grievance to her that Christopher enjoyed the consolations of the press in the course of his morning outing, but really his duality of impulse was all for the best. She might well have entered upon her final apathy several years earlier had her husband not had two strings for her to play on.

When the washing-up and the drying were done, Christopher Homm would fold his hands for a moment in a towel and then unwrap them still wet. He had dried the cups with the labour and precision of a man climbing a mountain, but now he was on the plateau and gazed on the promised land his concentration was less. He would go and get his newspaper.

He walked out of the kitchen sideways as if not wishing to leave his back exposed to his wife's stare. Felicia let him go till he was in the passage and his finger was on the latch of the door. At the first tiny click she shouted, in a voice that came from a cupboard:

"You're not out after that paper?"

Christopher Homm did not deny his crime but waited.

"And what about my shopping? I suppose you expect me to do all the clearing up here and then that as well?"

Christopher would be fool enough to suggest that that line of argument was unfair.

"I thought you said you could manage without the cocoa?"

Felicia took this point with great relish. "Ha! Without the cocoa, yes. But what about the other things? I'm just looking to see what I want."

The last three words were spoken in a voice increasingly muffled. It was as if Felicia were disappearing into a corner of the bottom shelf of her cupboard. It was Christopher's duty to stand in the hall with his hand on the latch until Felicia was ready with her shopping list. However remote might be the mouseholes she was scrabbling in, if Christopher opened the door to see what sort of day it was she would shout:

25

"You're not going without this list are you?"

Christopher would reply that he just wanted to see what sort of day it was.

"You can see that by looking out of the window."

But if Christopher, in order to look out of the front room window, withdrew from the door or even took his hand off the latch, Felicia would call out cheerfully:

"I'm ready now!"

Then Christopher had to renew his station by the door. This declaration of readiness was, however, often a feint. Felicia would come to meet Christopher in the hall, wearing a smile. Her lips would part to begin her catalogue of wants and then she might say:

"Oh! There is one thing more." And she would disappear again. His waiting would then begin once more.

At last Christopher Homm would be allowed to go. In the end there were never more than one or two things on the shopping list, for had there been more it would have become unnecessary to shop every day. Neither spouse could have borne that. By felicitous dispositions which in fact prevented any such revision of their arrangements, each retained a power to hurt the other. Life does not need joy, but it needs more common remedies against insensibility.

Yet as he made his escape, Christopher knew such approximations to joy as were left to him. His going was an act of obedience and yet almost of freedom. His contracting frame would not enable him to embrace his duty and make the freedom complete. He could not inhale the free wind of Torrington Street in such bursting lungfuls that there was no room in his heart for resentment against Felicia. None the less, as he crept on it was with what, had he been stronger, would have been exhilaration. He read the advertisement board; he bought his paper; if the newsagent were sprawling with his elbows on the counter, not utterly absorbed in a western or his account books, he even dared a comment about the weather.

"Nasty east wind blowing Mr Richards."

The newsagent was surly and, if he answered at all, it was to prove that the weather had unfavourable effects on newsagents but that no one else had a right to complain. The east wind was particularly piercing at seven o'clock when he set out on his rounds; it was comparatively balmy by the time Mr Homm ventured out. Fine, mild weather on the other hand, served only to impress Mr Richards with the inescapability of his servile condition, whereas to a man who had retired things were otherwise. To get the full relish of the contrast, and at the same time to avenge himself for the hardship he suffered, Mr Richards might add:

"And you're young enough to enjoy your retirement Mr Homm."

The newsagent was a juicy man, and he sprawled farther over the counter with a sort of inchoate vitality as he spoke. This frightened Homm and he shrank towards the door. If Mr Richards were feeling cheerful he would at this point offend his customer further by offering his postcards:

"I've got some new ones in. Beautiful pieces. Have a look."

The offer was made as a tribute to Homm's recently developed piety and supposed rejection of the flesh. Homm could not explain his theology, which secretly permitted such indulgences as he was still capable of, so he suffered the taunt.

The grocer's shop was the place of a hope so desperate that Christopher Homm hardly permitted himself to be aware of it. For here, until her husband had taken her off to Canada, he might have met with his daughter Susan and his two grandchildren. The party would first be detected by a pram left outside the shop. Going in, Homm would survey the backs of the waiting women. Susan was easy to find for she

27

was sure not to be still for very long. He would catch sight of her head in movement, with a profile inscribed with a pre-occupied annoyance as she turned and bent to restrain a child who was enacting a restless fantasy in a world of skirt-hems and knees.

"Stop it, Peter! Cynthia, I'll smack your bottom!"

Christopher Homm, without formulating a judgment, sided with the invisible children who were the objects of these threats. Their obscure world among the biscuit tins and shopping baskets seemed to him a blissful retreat. Their reck-less vigour was the admiration of his poor conserved powers. He liked, if he could, to bend and peep at them before their mother caught sight of him. He would make at them comic faces which were confessions of a shameless despair. When he did, they would usually hide in their mother's skirt and she, guessing the cause, would say without looking round:

"Is that your granddad playing the fool again?"

But when the shopping was over, and the family re-assembled on the pavement, there was no member of it who did not feel a momentary pleasure. Homm felt that to the passers-by he could no longer seem a poor old man as he stood talking familiarly to creatures of his own in whom the sap still flowed. This vanity apart, the presence of these animals enlivened him. Even Susan, slightly irritated as usual and anxious to be off, was a creature of living muscle from top to toe. The children took a riotous pleasure in disorganizing everything as they climbed into their pram, sure of the anger of their mother and of the suppressed approbation of their grandfather. Susan's moment of pleasure came when there was a momentary order and the pram moved off. She could then tell her father how she was faring.

This was an occasion for attempted revenge. She had hated the oppressions of Torrington Street and had fled from them. Now she would make her father sorry for the meanness in which he had brought her up. She took pleasure in describing the splendour of her life.

It did not amount to much. She had a washing machine. She was likely to have a television. But that wasn't quite the same thing as going up to the West End, which was what she really liked. She did not reveal the decline of Bert's enthusiasm for such outings; she merely searched her harassed days for whatever distinguished them from the life of Torrington Street. When Bert decided to take her to Canada, it was on the difference between that country and Torrington Street that she dwelt:

"The air is a good deal fresher out there for the kids than it is in Torrington Street. You have a chance."

"There isn't the smoke out there that there is here."

"You can get on. The houses aren't so poky either."

Where she meant to punish she only delighted. Christopher Homm saw a shackle knocked off his own body each time his daughter described, with improvements, some freedom or luxury she had freshly achieved or hoped shortly to enjoy. The day she told him about Canada his spirit sailed into the mists of the heavy Atlantic.

He would have told Felicia when he got home about Susan's plans. But she would not give him an opening.

"I saw Sue and the kids today," he began tentatively.

Felicia sensed that he might have news. She was not going to have anyone stealing a march on her like that.

"Sue ought to do her shopping earlier. With two kids like that."

Then she put on her hat and hurried out to find at first hand what foolishness her daughter was planning.

IV

BEFORE HIS RETIREMENT CHRISTOPHER HOMM HAD
worked in a shoe warehouse, and it was in these vast caverns
that he had found God. Only the dimmest of lights, suspended from lofty and invisible ceilings, aided his search, but
the gloom hindered his spiritual quest less than it did his
quest for the shoes he needed to make up his orders. Indeed
it was in the gloom and interstices between the high piles of
boxes that he found reflected that emptiness of his own mind
which convinced him of his final dependence. He would walk
down the avenues of stock, his spectacles slipping a little down
his nose, his pencil behind his ear, and his hands deep in the
pockets of his long khaki coat. He would stop to pry among
the numbers on the ends of the boxes and, when he came to
a gap, he would thrust his nose and his spectacles a little
further forward to make sure that there was nothing concealed from him in a recess. When he found nothing, the
sudden release from the monotony of numbers was as much
a happiness as a disappointment. He did not discourse with
himself of these impressions, but whenever he was unoccupied
for ten minutes the recollections of these little happinesses
collected in his mind till they were big enough to form a
hope.

The hope would never have taken the form it did had not
Felicia, partly to secure him from the less reputable ways he
had once followed and partly to give an importance to
herself, induced him to become a regular attendant at the
little chapel with which he had long had a tenuous connexion. It was the only time, in these years, that she had
praised him:

"I'm sure you could pray as well as some of them that stand up there."

And when he had ventured:

"You should do it a bit louder. They won't pay any attention to you unless you speak loud."

Under this tuition, Christopher Homm tied the little mysteries of his warehouse to the oratorical practices of the chapel. It gave him a chance to renew his youth by stirring memories of political strife. The only logical talk he had ever known had been of politics. If a man got on his feet to talk, that was what it must be about. If a man had a fire for things beyond the flesh, it must be in some manner for those things. It was thus that Christopher Homm began to report publicly to God on all those items of news which could be made to look morally uplifting.

The warehouse was the scene for years of the daily hesitations of his heart and pencil. He always spoke after he left of having retired, but it was never entirely clear to his conscience that he had not been given the sack.

"You keep on there," Felicia would say when he talked of giving up. "We can do with the money. Besides, what would I do with you at home all day?"

So Christopher, however tired he might grow, would hardly have dared deliberately to give up. Instead, over several years and particularly in the final months, he found himself behaving with an increasing recklessness, which was bound in the end to lead to his losing his job. He looked a careful man, for his face was as sad as his solid khaki coat, and for a time this made his errors incredible. When the vanman shouted to the Office that that old fool had brought him three dozen sixes instead of two dozen fives, the Office was inclined to think, in spite of all evidence, that Christopher Homm was being maligned. Christopher looked pathetic as he trotted past the glass partition which separated the Office from the warehouse. The pile of boxes looked too heavy for him and always on the point of toppling over.

"Poor old Homm," the short puffy man who was in charge of the office would say.

Christopher Homm was furious to find himself the object of so much forgiveness. He was no longer a demonstrative man, and he had no words but mumbled ones in reply to the vanman's abuse. He appeared, therefore, to Mr Wilson looking out of the office window, to be conducting himself with exemplary patience. Mr Wilson, who was a gardener not a religious man, even remarked one Sunday morning to his wife, in order to delay a little longer the moment when he was sent out to dig in the icy wind:

"It's surprising how old Homm at the warehouse puts up with those vanmen cursing and swearing at him. It almost makes you wonder if there isn't something in this turning the other cheek. He's a great chapel-goer you know."

Mrs Wilson made no reply but indicated the gardening boots, and she was right, for as so often there was nothing in the theory her husband was adumbrating. Mr Wilson had in time to admit this.

When Chrisopher Homm discovered that a simple error in an order attracted only Mr Wilson's charity, he started to do worse. His first ruse was to send the pile of boxes he was carrying toppling over just as he passed the office door. Mr Wilson at once rushed out and helped to pick them up. He didn't like to see the boxes damaged but his first thought was that Homm was carrying too many:

"Take a few less, old chap. He can wait while you make a second journey."

Christopher received this with a disdain that looked like submissiveness, and next time passed with a bigger pile and sent that flying. Mr Wilson was much concerned.

"There really is no need for such hurry, old chap. I meant what I said about bringing only half that lot."

Poor old fellow, he thought, he's afraid I'll think he's past it and give him the sack. But Christopher was fuming because it seemed that he could not displease. He reverted to his first plan of bringing the wrong pile and, when the error was discovered, he brought it back again and again. Then Mr Wilson began to think that, after all, Homm was getting past it. But he could not be brutal about a matter like that. Next Sunday morning, which was wet as well as cold, he tried to discuss the matter with his wife:

"You know I told you about old Homm. I'm afraid he's getting past it."

"Is that the old man you said about turning the other cheek?" Mrs Wilson asked. "I should think he was."

Mr Wilson was not going to have his comfortable discourse in front of the gas-fire cut short by mere agreement. He ignored the boots that his wife pushed towards him with her toe.

"It's a very sad thing when an old man begins to break up like that." He told of Homm's errors and accidents.

"I shall think that you're beginning to break up if you carry on like that," said Mrs Wilson. "You'll never get that digging done."

Mr Wilson sighed, more for himself than for Christopher Homm, and as he put on his boots said with an air of importance:

"It's a problem I shall have to tackle."

It was. In the week that followed Homm's behaviour became fantastic. He was like a clown who sought to amuse by solemn misconceptions. He climbed a ladder and put a pile of boxes down in mid-air as on a shelf. He brought children's shoes instead of ladies' in contradiction of Mr Wilson's own express and carefully worded orders. It was this last wild mistake which led the Office to conclude at last that the confusion must be wilful. It was unlikely that anyone could misunderstand Mr Wilson's lucidly expressed orders. And this time Homm's mutterings were audible.

"You ought to make yourself clear Mr Wilson."

Mr Wilson was clear. He said incredulously:

"I what?"

At this Homm saw the possibility of a final scene. He raised his voice and smiled:

"You want to be a bit clearer when you give orders. You want to say what you mean."

Mr Wilson saw that something was afoot. When Homm had come to him years before, people had said:

"He's an insolent devil. You'll never do anything with him."

For years he had waited obscurely for a manifestation. Now when he had forgotten he was waiting, this was it. Mr Wilson began to recollect, though less with his mind than with his body, his own past. He had had a temper, a healthy joyful affair, and he had grown too sluggish for such pleasures. But now his blood began to move round steadily and with delicious pulsations. He stared at Homm with utter patience until his emotions were ready. Then quite suddenly he shouted:

"I won't have anyone talk like that to me, see? If I don't make myself clear, no-one does."

It was a real pleasure to talk so loudly. Christopher Homm obliged him by inciting him further. Christopher was blissful now; he saw his release. He put on his praying face and said as if in the presence of a public:

"Ah, you can lie and deceive yourself when it suits you. The working man of this country won't stand for that sort of thing for ever."

"Get away from this office, Homm! Get away from this

34

office!" Mr Wilson was benign and majestic. He saw now what he had to do. Homm could not remain.

It was with reluctance that Homm disengaged from this action, for he was not absolutely sure that he had won his point. But he knew that all was well when in the middle of the afternoon Wilson sent for him and gave him two weeks' pay.

"You've been here a long time, Homm, and there'll be a bit more to come. But I don't want to see you here again."

The two men smiled at one another, each in the extremest pleasure he had known for years. Mr Wilson was conscious of a renewal of animal vigour. Christopher Homm enjoyed a sentiment of liberty as he was about to enter upon a great servitude.

Susan was paying a call when he got home. That added to the splendour and force of his announcement:

"I've retired," he said, sitting down in the armchair like a master.

Felicia took up this gauntlet at once. She had had premonitions.

"How do you suppose I'm going to manage without that money? You sit there like a king and you don't care."

Christopher Homm was a king, but his reign was short. Felicia stormed his throne with her tears.

"You selfish old man! You never said a word about it. Here I scrape and save and you just throw away your job."

Susan was standing there with something more like detachment than one would have thought her capable of. Her sympathies did not extend to the crawling passions of old people, and for the moment she did not see how her own interests were affected.

"Oh mum, maybe he couldn't help it," she said, for all her indifference a little scandalized at this attack on what looked like a misfortune.

"He never told me a thing about it," said Felicia. That was his greatest crime. Her breasts wobbled with weeping. "I never know where I am with him. Don't sit there smiling, Chris."

He was not going to do so much longer. The smile was growing thin and painful. He had begun to see that even in this situation he could not be master.

"He just laughs at me," Felicia shrieked, determined to drive the last symptoms of pleasure from her husband's face. "Oh Sue, you're all right with Bert but if you knew all I've had to put up with all these years. If it wasn't for me he wouldn't be here even."

Sue did know, if obscurely. The mutual torture of her parents' life had corrupted her childhood. It had further darkened the already architectural gloom of Torrington Street for eighteen years.

"Oh shut up, mum. For God's sake don't start that!"

Felicia then insisted that her daughter too had turned against her. No-one, it seemed, had ever given that exalted wife and mother her due. This was the kind of talk that made Susan feel sick. She started to go, but her mother boo-hooed more vociferously than ever. Felicia said that they would end with their heads in the gas-oven. Evidently she had no intention of putting her own head in and leaving her husband to triumph. Susan obscurely seized this point, for she felt suddenly sure that things were not so bad as her mother made out. She decided she could leave her parents to it if she first made them a cup of tea. The performance of this service gave her the relief of escape to the kitchen. As she filled the kettle and got out the cups she felt as she did when she managed to put a closed door between herself and the kids.

When she re-entered the sitting room Homm was mumbling explanations. She could see at once that he was now the beaten contestant. That satisfied her, for she knew that no row could end until her father admitted defeat, and that most rows in time blew over when he did.

"Get me a couple of aspirins, there's a dear." Felicia's tone was calm now.

"I don't know when I've been so upset," Mrs Homm went on as Susan came back with the aspirins. Her daughter, however, had no difficulty in recalling scenes equally tempestuous. She left the old woman to her tea and her drugs.

"I'll look in on Thursday," she said. When she did, the argument between her parents had taken the more abstract and enduring form of a social combat. Her father was saying, in what was little more than a mutter:

"A working man has a right to a bit of rest at the end of his days as well as anyone else."

And her mother was saying sharply, not in logical reply but in counterpoint:

"Middle class people like us are going to find it very difficult to make ends meet on what we got."

V

ONE OF FELICIA'S PLEASURES IN LIFE WAS TO GET
her daughter to cook her a bit of hot dinner. If the occasion
were to be as formal and as burdensome to Sue as Mrs Homm
desired it should be, it was necessary that Christopher should
go too and this meant, so long as he was still working, that it
must be on a Sunday. This was, anyhow, the day on which
the scene could be set with most splendour. Sue could then
spend the morning preparing the meal while Christopher
and Felicia prepared their stomachs by protracted prayers.
Moreover, Sunday being the day for best clothes, there was
on that day something more than usually impressive about
the old people's appearance. Christopher wore his grey suit
and white collar, in which he could hardly bend, so that,
humble though he was, he had at least the stiffness of majesty.
Felicia was in her navy blue. Her main structure had rather
the appearance of a tall house of that colour. The roof was
the jutting stretch from her neck to the utmost point of her
bosom. The wall was what fell perpendicularly from there.
Her head was a grotesque chimney-pot. But it was not
merely in order to astonish with her architecture that
Felicia liked to wear her best clothes when she visited Susan.
A more practical point was that, in her best clothes, she could
not help. She had to sit smiling in an armchair, which was
not only more agreeable but allowed her to spend her whole
force in speech and other electrical messages indicating her
pleasure and the imperatives of good house-keeping. Christopher so far did off his majesty as to crawl with his grandchildren in the world under the table, which he preferred
to that on top. His bony quarters would usually be sticking

out under the table-cloth when Bert came in from the garden. Bert would first be heard washing his hands in the kitchen. He always timed his arrival to coincide with the moment when Susan was straining the vegetables. The two clashed ferociously at the sink. On these occasions they always said the same things to one another; why must you get in my way and you want to have vegetables don't you. Bert was surly, all back and fore-arms; Susan agitated, all twisted fingers and screwed-up mouth. When Bert had, if at all possible, initiated a final hysteria by flicking soap into the gravy, he marched into the dining room to fall over his father-in-law's heels.

Bert did not put on his best suit to have a bit of hot dinner with the old people. He made it a point of superiority not to dress up on Sundays unless in the most sporty clothes. The check tweed jacket and the blue shirt were, however, for afternoon wear. At dinner-time he preferred to stick to his working shirt and trousers to show that he had not been wasting his morning yodelling and belly-aching at the chapel. Bert was what you might call an advanced thinker.

As Bert sat down with the *News of the World* in the arm-chair opposite his mother-in-law he would if at all possible make his joke. This consisted, more particularly if he had succeeded in falling pretty heavily over Christopher's heels, of saying as he sat down:

"So you left Dad singing hymns?"

This was Felicia's cue to reason with her husband on the impropriety of grovelling on the floor, first, in his best clothes, and secondly with the children when Bert had come in and Christopher hadn't even noticed him. Having set the pair of them off on a quarrel, Bert would open the paper and lose himself in its fantasies. Though he liked the spicy bits and read them first, he did not dawdle over them for he was a student of football and the sports page had to be read so that at dinner-time he could make conversation on matters not of general interest.

Susan finally came in wiping her hands in her apron, shouted at the children to come up from under the table or she would make them so sore they couldn't sit down. Christopher knew that this was intended for him, if not as a physical threat at least as a reproach, and he came out as quickly as he could and said "Hullo Bert" as if to give the impression that he had just arrived from outside. Felicia then took a turn at cajoling the children, which she did not do directly but in such terms as were a correction to her daughter. All except Bert would then take their places, and Bert had to be specially prayed to come out from behind his newspaper. This he at last did with affected surprise, and took his seat at the head of the table. No sooner was Sue instructing him how to carve the joint than he, as a counter-blast, began to discourse on what he had just learned about Saturday's football. The conversation would be:

"A bit of brown off the top for Cynthia. No leave that not that a bit from the other side."

"The Spurs played a good game yesterday."

"You know it's no good giving Peter fat."

"I knew Preston would never make it; they're not up to much this season."

With these elegant expressions the young people gave one another appetite and indigestion. They did not exchange thoughts, even the simplest, but each, in turn or out of turn, as it were fired a rocket at a central point in the ceiling. Only the children made a little savage community, the excesses of which were intermittently excited by violent words from Sue and thick ears from Bert until each of the children too was driven into a complete isolation of shrieks and bellows.

When the moral chaos was thus complete, and no one person in the room any longer had even any contact with any

40

other, Bert would sometimes decide that the moment had come for him to exercise a portentous rôle. So long as he could touch the minds of others, however gormlessly, he was doubtful of his own rights and authority, but in the inspiration of rage he became a judge.

In these moments it needed no special demeanour on the part of his son to exercise the full wrath. The mere continuation of the habitual messiness and incompetence was enough. Suddenly Bert would lean forward, seize Pete by the scruff of his neck and throw him on to the floor. The boy then howled louder, and Susan began to scream too, not against brutality but against what she considered an interruption of hygienic feeding.

"That boy hasn't eaten a thing. You ought to have more sense, Bert. What do you think I spend the morning cooking dinner for?"

At this Felicia would range herself against Susan. After all, this was a bit thick. Had not the dinner been cooked for *her*?

"There's five of us to eat up the dinner even if Pete won't," she said magnificently.

"If the little bugger can't behave he shan't eat." Bert had at the back of his mind an expression, the sense of which he did not in all circumstances approve, about those who don't work. But no meanings were now of any consequence. Bert was warming up for an orgy below the surface of words. To reach the pitch of further action he required incitement, and at the moment she saw him sinking back into lethargy Susan would give it.

"Don't you touch that boy at dinner time! Don't you touch him now! Get on with your dinner."

This was enough. Bert rose from his chair and drove Peter from the room. The two could be heard mounting the stairs, Peter crying for mercy.

Bert in this mood was not the man to give the boy a whack and have done with it. This was a ceremony.

"Sue, where's that stick?" he would shout down the stairs, and Sue would go to the cupboard and take out a thin cane. She would hand it up the stairs and sit down again, calm now and with a smile, like a woman whose meal has been interrupted by the baker calling.

"It's such a nuisance just at dinner-time," she would say.

Above the heads of the dinner party was the noise of a slight scuffle and then of three or four cuts of the cane. Pete sobbed, and Bert slowly descended the stairs and took his place at the head of the table. It was the most benign moment of the party. The two parents were relaxed as from a mutual pleasure. Their limbs seemed beautifully weighted and balanced. Their lips were half opened in a smile.

Christopher Homm smiled into the general relaxation. He did not expect this world to be a place of gentleness, and he would have been grateful for the momentary peace by whatever evil it might have been purchased. He could now ask Bert how the garden was. Then when dinner was over, he and Bert would go to the back door to look at it, leaving the women to admire Bert's violence and cooingly to deplore both men and children.

The garden was small and meticulously kept. A concrete path divided it lengthways, and a ferocious sense of order had guided Bert to marshal Michaelmas daisies and roses in equal squares on either side of the door. The rest of the garden, beautifully dug and hoed, was given over to rows of various vegetables. The two men would stop to admire each row, Bert explaining for each how he had improved on nature and precedent.

It was when this was over that Christopher Homm achieved his full stature. He could for the first time during his visit be seen to be magisterial. Bert, who before the women made a point of showing contempt for his father-in-law, now spoke to him in soft masculine tones with something like deference.

"I'm a bit tired of life here, Dad," he would begin diffidently. Christopher would smile the smile of one who had lived through all this, and much more. It was the much more that impressed Bert.

"You was a bit of a lad once, not so long ago neither," he said enviously. Christopher Homm's face showed first shame at what was attributed to him, then pleasure at the recollection, and lastly the simpering malevolence of one taking credit for evil performed.

"You don't want to follow the way I went Bert," he said. "You stick to Sue and the kids."

A world of evil shimmered before Bert's eyes like a lake. There was no crime or delight that he would not bathe in if he were free.

Christopher Homm could have said that the liberty he had followed had brought him nothing. But by that confession he would only have reverted once more to being the object of Bert's contempt. He therefore continued to smile, saying little and taking credit for his vices, and hoping that Bert would think them more splendid than they had in fact been.

"Of course I seen a thing or two."

"I bet you did, Dad.

Christopher Homm felt happy. As a prophet and exponent of evil, he could at that moment have returned to the chapel and spoken about evil till nobody knew whether he was for or against it. It was a lonely joy, for the mind of Bert, soaring to its own isolation, had already left him.

It was after one of these performances in the garden that Bert, feeling that if evil failed him he could as a second best at least try to be distinguished for good, first mooted with Sue the project of going to Canada. He saw himself, a figure

43

of tremendous energy, felling with a sickle to right and left of him acres of wheat and the toppling skyscrapers of millionaire industrial enterprises. He would be that kind of demon.

And Christopher would say, as he and his wife walked home to Torrington Street:

"That was a nice bit of hot dinner Sue gave us. '

VI

THERE WERE OCCASIONS WHEN CHRISTOPHER HOMM'S
respectability seemed to have been imposed upon him by a
not altogether successful act of policy. Never was this more
the case than when he stood leering and snickering among the
guests after Sue's wedding. He was wearing his best suit; he
even had a rose in his buttonhole. But the smarter his outer
covering the grimier his face looked. The more his suit
resembled a carapace, the more his face betrayed a moral
uncertainty needing to be sustained or disguised. Felicia stood
by him like a warden. The young couple, too, had the look
of captives, prisoners less of one another than of entangling
circumstances. None of these appearances was a lie.

The whole occasion was a triumph of respectability. It was
Felicia's day. She might herself have arranged the tensions
of everyone's muscles and the folds of their clothes. She had
constructed this ordered event from a chaos which had almost
dissolved her family. Christopher Homm lived, however
quietly, on the very frontiers of order. It was wholly due to
Felicia that he was to be found on the right side of those
frontiers, or even physically to be found at all, when he was
needed to give away his daughter and to pose or strut for a
moment before the camera and so to provide a trophy of
propriety for Susan's and for Felicia's front-room mantel-
pieces. As for Bert and Susan, who, if not the centre of this
splendid scene at any rate played a rôle which could not be
dispensed with, it was Felicia, certainly, who had brought
them to this celebration.

From being a tentative and feared possibility the thing
had become an objective from the moment she had become

certain that Bert had been messing about with Susan. Felicia never doubted her ability to bring off any plan she once seriously entertained. In this matter she felt, in the end, that Bert had played into her hands.

Susan had tried to escape from the oppressions of Torrington Street. It was difficult to make an excuse for going out in the evening which could not be questioned till it was denuded of both propriety and feasibility. Susan therefore came home late. Felicia had prepared a damaging question:

"I suppose you've been doing overtime again? The money will be useful at the end of the week."

Susan saw that she could not purchase liberty with so easy a lie. Her mother knew what her savings were, so she would shortly have to admit that she had not earned the extra money.

"You don't understand, mum," she said, "We don't get overtime till the week after we worked it like."

The pay-day came, however. By really doing overtime twice in the next fortnight, Susan had designed to conceal her one night of truancy. But by the time the money came Felicia had made herself the master of the system of payment. She knew when the pay was made up, what the hourly rate and the overtime rates were. Susan bought herself a pair of shoes and hoped, by lying about the price, to make her sums come right.

"But you said six hours overtime altogether and that comes to such and such."

"Yes, but the shoes mum. They cost forty-five shillings and I put some of the overtime money towards that."

"You never paid forty-five for them," said Felicia suspiciously. Susan was driven to protest that she did. She was compelled to say where she had got them.

"I'll speak to the manager there. I think it's robbery," said Felicia, testing the ground further.

Susan became alarmed.

"I'll go in first thing tomorrow morning," Felicia went on. "I've got to go that way."

She could see that she was torturing Susan now, and she felt that she was on the right track.

"First thing tomorrow morning.

"It'll be interesting to hear what they got to say.

"I expect that they have got things just as good at two-thirds of the price."

These sentences were emitted by Felicia at intervals throughout the evening. Whenever she saw the cracks in Susan's defences closing up she would take out one of her sentences and prise them open again. At last Susan confessed.

"So you were telling lies. You went out to the pictures. Who did you go with?"

In spite of her strenuous lies about the shoes the weakest point in Susan's defences was her habit of telling the truth. She admitted it was not with one of the girls from the work-room that she had gone out with but one of the chaps from the factory down the road. What was his name?

"They call him Bert," she said. "I don't know his proper name."

Felicia could in any case have seen that a chap they called Bert could not be the son-in-law for her. But her daughter's admission that she did not even know his proper name filled her with fury.

"You stand there and tell me that," she said. "I never thought I'd live to see a daughter of mine a street walker."

Felicia ceased to attend to her daughter and performed excursions of rage and pity over herself. She was deserted by Susan. It was not merely that her daughter was walking out; she was picking up men in the street. It was her dad coming out in her. There could be no more wounding accusation than that.

Susan replied that Bert never touched her and Felicia, who knew her daughter's truthful habit, was disappointed. She was not to be given occasion to carry her questioning into the interesting and deplorable pastures of sex.

For this pleasure she had, however, not long to wait. If lying was too difficult Susan, who was not to be denied a girl's vanity, would stay out and make no excuses. She did.

Felicia had felt so certain of the good effects of her first row about Bert that at the next deliberate defection on the part of Susan she was incredulous and almost quiet. This emboldened the girl, who the following night came in at eleven o'clock with a saucy air.

"Where have you been?"

"Oh, I've been out with my young man."

"Your young man? Is it that Bert chap you picked up before?"

Susan replied that of course it was Bert, and added with assurance that he wasn't just a chap but had in fact a surname.

"We all got that," said Felicia pulling her lips tight. "But he can still mess about with you." This time Susan was silent, and Felicia was quick to notice that there was no denial.

"So he has been, has he?" She smiled in triumph as well as anger.

"He has been what, mother?" said Susan. "I don't know what you're talking about."

Her mother made it plain what she was talking about. But her tongue was more daring than Bert's hands. She made such accusations as Susan was again able to deny.

Gradually, by a slow pressure against Felicia's will, Bert came to be accepted as Susan's young man. He even came to tea on a series of Sunday afternoons, and was in the end left with Susan in the half-darkened front room when Felicia went off to chapel. The hard sofa, with the cushions and

48

covers always sliding off on to the floor, was the scene of the combats in which Bert drew near to his objective. Susan was in her summer dress with the scantiest of underwear when Bert finally took her. After that, on Sunday evenings when Felicia prayed, Bert regularly assailed her daughter. A failure in his precautions led to Susan turning to her mother in alarm.

Felicia listened to the news of her daughter's suspected pregnancy with a great calm. This was, after all, an ancestral occasion. The anger a mother must feel at first handing her child over to another's embraces had been spent on the first encounter. Felicia had now only to glory in the responsibility of having the child once more pliant between her hands. Moreover, if she had made a practice of leaving Sue alone with Bert it was not until, summing the young man up, she had made up her mind that she could deal with him. Now, if need be, she would.

Need was not. Bert, for his part, had also summed up Felicia and he knew that he must have the worse in any direct encounter.

"It's all right, dear," he said to Susan. "You tell your ma we'll get married."

Marrying just now had been no part of Bert's rational plans, but he admitted to himself that he had asked for it and that he was without an answer should Mrs Homm choose to be indignant. He didn't really see why Susan shouldn't get rid of her baby, in the early stages it wasn't really anything. He meant to put this to her, but when her candid eyes were on him he was prevented from doing so by a fear which he did not identify but which might have been shame.

It was thus that the wedding party came to be assembled. The thing was done in all the more splendour because Felicia knew it would not be long before neighbours were saying that you could see now why Susan Homm had had to get married. Felicia felt that it would magically warn off the approaching scandal if there were nothing hole-and-corner about the wedding arrangements. So, on the day, white-ribboned cars dashed up and down Torrington Street. There was a reception in the little hall behind the Chapel. Sandwiches and lemonade, fancies as well as home-made cakes, and cups of tea from an urn were set out on a trestle table, and there was malicious satisfaction on every chapel-going lip that the bridegroom who was the occasion of this should look so hopelessly uncomfortable.

"Of course, he's never been near the place before. He must feel strange."

"I don't think I've ever seen Bert at any of the services."

"Now you're married you'll have to bring him along."

"Perhaps we'll see you here sometimes now with Susan."

Bert dared not even choke in his desperation. It seemed as if the reception would never end. He did not, at this stage, know his father-in-law well enough deliberately to seek comfort in that quarter. And Christopher himself, who at least was known at the chapel in a vague way if not admired, was himself not happy. He found ease in stooping behind the tea-urn, turning the tap and tilting it, performances which enabled him not to meet the eyes of the guests.

"You're just at the beginning of life now," he said to Bert in threatening tones as the latter drew near in order to hide his face by pretending to help.

Bert made the rueful sounds of one unwilling to admit an embarrassing truth. He disliked the reproof, but he felt safer in the company of his father-in-law and the tea-urn than of his bride and her matrons of prey. As Christopher felt the young man drawing nearer he became bolder himself and an anxiety that had been inhabiting him like a spirit suddenly came out of his mouth in fierce words:

"You look after Sue, or I'll smash your face in."

Bert was astonished and a little admiring at this sudden access of energy in an old man he regarded as beaten and effete. Christopher, for his part, immediately after the words had escaped him felt the need to be conciliatory. He looked around as if for suggestions as to how he might be so without alluding again to the occasion of his offence. His eye fell on the open side door of the hall, and he suddenly felt strong with a conspiratorial courage.

"Bert," he said, "come out this way a minute."

They found themselves in a yard with a dustbin and the drainpipes. Christopher put forward his tremendous suggestion.

"What about going and having one? They'll be open now."

A few yards away rose the blank red-brick of the public-house wall. They could go out of the side gate and be in the bar in a moment.

Bert felt that the crime was huge, less for himself than for Christopher. He felt he ought to ask his father-in-law whether he had considered what Mrs Homm would say about it. But he was too glad to be out to let this charity drive out his thirst or the pleasure it gave him to grin a wicked assent.

The barman looked at Christopher with surprise:

"Well Mr Homm it's quite a time since we seen you down here."

Christopher blushed, not for his crime but because it was publicly noticed that he had fallen from the evil ways he had so long honourably followed. He tried to make out that he was still a free man.

"Oh, I like a drink now and again. What'll you have, Bert?"

Had Bert remembered that this was his wedding-day he would have been smart and had some expensive drink, but he was aware only of his hot and fibrous body from which all liquid seemed to have been drained. He asked for a pint and poured it into himself as into the radiator of a motor-car. It was only with the second pint that he began to reflect.

There, leaning against the bar, was his astonishing father-in-law, his sad dry face a little flushed and his hair limp and errant. Over the lips which should have been those of a subdued man played the flicker of an amused, contemptuous passion.

"Well, boy, you'll soon know what it is," said the old man without further explanation.

Bert moved uneasily and felt young. He had big bones, clad like a hippopotamus's with flesh that gave the impression of being armour. His cheeks were notably flat and solid and he had thick lips to set off his ludicrous moustache.

"What'll I know?" asked Bert with a trace of fight, and the barman, thinking the point a simpler one than it was, winked.

The derision on Christopher Homm's face became more patent and offensive.

"You'll know the bloody sweat of life my boy."

Bert murmured that he knew a thing or two already but Christopher Homm obviously did not accept that.

"When the little bastards come along there won't be no more going to football."

"Won't there, though, we'll see."

"We'll see, all right," replied Christopher. "You're going to be a respectable citizen now. You don't know what that means."

The limitations of meanness and carnality had always enclosed Bert in a cage he understood to be respectability, and his father-in-law's menacing irony merely puzzled him. He understood better the change of countenance that followed and the repetition of the warning:

"But mind what I said about Sue!"

52

In this less equivocal mood Christopher Homm led the way out of the bar and back to the chapel hall, where Felicia wobbled with rage and re-conquered him without a word. Bert sought out Sue:

"Your Dad's a funny old sport," he said. "He took me out for a drink."

Sue was still close enough to her home to glower at the thought of what domestic rages must follow. And indeed, while the young couple were on the honeymoon Felicia was almost wholly occupied with re-educating Christopher.

VII

IT WAS NOT MERELY FROM TWO PINTS OF BEER THAT
Felicia was re-educating Christopher. She feared a recrudes-
cence of greater evils. Within herself she carried an historical
fear. It was the imperfection of Christopher's love that had
twisted her into a permanent fear of his aberration. The
wedding of Susan and Bert had not only repaired, at any
rate temporarily and superficially, the disorder in her family
caused by Susan's defection and illicit yielding; it had been
the occasion of the resumption of her own show of matrimony. For to celebrate the wedding she had brought Christopher Homm home from a long desertion.

When she had first become certain that her hard front-
room sofa had been the theatre of her daughter's deflowering
she had come to a resolution concerning herself. What she
had of consciousness was occupied with her design of bringing Bert to acknowledge that the appetite of his flesh had
committed him to a more formal husbandry. At the same
time, however, that slower but yet more resolute will which
does not need a mind had achieved a decision of its own. It
may in some sort have been that the secret preparations of
this will had led her to indulge the young couple with privacy
to a degree which made their enjoyment a certainty.

However that may be, this secret collection of Felicia's
forces propelled her into the street one Monday morning,
wearing her best clothes and a face that was bland with
certainty. She was going to look for her husband, who had
left her several years before almost at the same time as
Susan had started work.

Felicia had hitherto been too much injured by Christopher's defection to take any active steps to retrieve him or, her neighbours and even her daughter might have said, so much as to notice his departure. Without even deigning to make any enquiries, or publicly to give ear to the gossip about him, she had however noted and retained every tiniest clue as to his whereabouts. She knew he was still working at the same establishment as before and had gone no further away to live than was necessary to keep out of her sight so long as she confined herself to her customary perambulations. Christopher knew his wife's pride and felt sure that she would not humiliate herself by looking for him. It needed another distress to give her that weakness or that courage.

In case her quest should fail, Felicia even now took precautions to make sure that no neighbour should suspect her of it. Her best clothes were put on less to astonish her husband than to lead her neighbours and if possible even herself to think that she was going up to town to look at the shops. To give colour to this illusion, she made her way to the usual bus-stop and bought a ticket expensive enough to take her all the way to town. But when she had ridden only three-pennyworth she got off and began to walk along the pavement. She was as troubled to dispose of the bus ticket which registered her deception as a murderer might be to dispose of a body. She twisted it, and shredded it into tiny pieces, but would not leave her traces by dropping it on the paving stones. At last, when she thought no-one was looking, she popped it into a litter bin. Then she turned off the main road into a side street.

The street was little different in architecture from the one from which she had set out. The houses seemed closely packed rather than merely contiguous, and they flanked the almost deserted road without grace. They were, however, evidently inhabited by persons of less constancy than those of Torrington Street. The curtains at the windows were not merely grimy, but carelessly hung and had holes in them. Even on a Monday morning the front rooms seemed to be in use. Too many people lived in these houses for any tenant to keep an empty sanctuary for respectability.

Felicia walked on with a determined step but without any plan or overt intention. At the first intersections of the streets she turned and continued her walk parallel with the main road. She encountered nothing but a cat and a milk cart.

So she continued from eleven in the morning till past three in the afternoon, turning at almost every corner and never telling herself what she was looking for. At last she found herself in the main road again and near her home. She went home quietly and took off her best clothes lest Susan should enquire where she had been. On Tuesday she stayed within doors and was angry with herself but on Wednesday she was once more out on her search. All day she prowled in the same network of streets, which she knew concealed her husband's hiding-place. It was growing dark when she resolved to ask a question. She would not enter a shop for there she would feel caged with her shame if the shop-keeper understood and smiled. It was an errand boy about to remount his bicycle that she questioned:

"You don't happen to know where Mr Homm lives, sonny?"

In the diffidence of its form and manner of delivery, the words were more like Christopher's than Felicia's. This was the moment of Felicia's greatest humility. Usually on the verge of indignation, at that moment she would not have been astonished if the boy had slapped her face or jumped on to his bicycle and ridden jeering away. It would have astonished her if he had shouted over the roof tops that here was Felicia Homm defeated by her husband and begging for mercy. But the boy said:

"Oh yes. Mr Homm is the back room in No. 29."

The humiliation had been unnecessary, for as the boy made off Christopher Homm turned the corner and advanced along the pavement towards her. There was no-one else to be seen. A meeting was inevitable.

Homm came slowly and smoothly like a blind man. He was in his working clothes under an old raincoat. As he came up to Felicia she thought he still had not seen her but there was a slight flush on his cheek and his eyes were an evasive blue.

As he passed he raised his hat, but his face did not relent. Felicia could not believe it. Within her great bulk a fire burned. She would not call Chris. She meant to hurry away, but stood still following him with her eyes. A few yards along the street, at number twenty-nine, he paused and turned in at the gate. In a moment he would be gone.

But it was the turn of Christopher for some modification of the automatic conduct he had followed. In the first shock and terror of seeing Felicia he had marched on because his body took him. Now a formed thought began to prise open his consciousness. He turned and looked at his wife. When he saw she was still looking at him it became impossible any longer to play the game of isolation. It was as if they were in a room together. So gradually that at first the direction of his movement was doubtful, Christopher turned again and moved slowly back along the pavement.

Neither of the two had any word ready when they at last confronted one another. Christopher could not speak, and Felicia would not for fear of making a confession. At length Christopher gathered a few words and scattered them again:

"What are you doing here, Lissy?"

"I just come down this way and happened to see you."

"How did you know it was here I lived?"

"I didn't know, I just come down this way."

There was a long pause and Christopher began to wonder how he could extricate himself. The distance back to number twenty-nine seemed longer than he could ever walk. Then Felicia, as if realizing that she might lose him again, said:

"It's about Sue."

Christopher Homm did not answer but Felicia could see that she had his attention.

"You know a chap called Bert at the factory down the road? He's been messing about with her."

The face of Christopher Homm changed to a deep and angry colour. The poor skin that sagged over tired muscles stretched to make room for their rejuvenate working.

"I'll smash his face in for'n."

There was an unusual rusticity about his accent. He did not say any more, but he did not move away. Felicia was pleased with him.

"He's been messing about with her Sundays and she's in the family way."

Mrs Homm watched with satisfaction the working of her propaganda. When she judged that the moment had come she said slily:

"It wants a man to deal with him. I can't do nothing."

She affected this weakness. Bert had already succumbed to the terror exercised by his future mother-in-law.

Christopher began to walk down the street in the direction of the bus for Torrington Street. Felicia accompanied him a few yards, pleased with her success but a prey now of another anxiety.

"Hadn't you better get a few things, Chris?"

The mind of Christopher Homm was filled with one thing. He had not asked himself where he would sleep that night. He did not know he was changing his address and, if he had known, he would not have cared for the fate of his belongings.

"I don't have to have anything," he said stubbornly.

But Felicia was regaining her ascendancy.

"It won't take a minute just to put a few things in a case like."

It was a risk for him to go back to number twenty-nine. Felicia did not know whose lair it was. Some woman's, perhaps. But Felicia had only to look once at Christopher to see that both his colour and his resolution had gone. He would not disobey her. She left him to go by himself to fetch his old suitcase. He came back in less than five minutes with the case bulging and tied up with a piece of webbing.

It had been too easy. Felicia could scarcely repress her scorn for the captive. There was no talk of Susan now and in her confidence Felicia made plans instead for her own honeymoon.

"They say that's a good picture," she said as they passed the cinema. "We might go, Chris."

Christopher Homm said nothing. He was still worrying, obscurely, about his daughter, but that deep horror was being overlaid by a consciousness that Felicia had been too good for him. He was still uncertain why he had come with her, when Felicia took out her key and let him in to number ninety-two Torrington Street. It was she who came in second and closed the door.

"Sue," she called out. "I've got your Dad here." Christopher Homm was certain now he was not the hero who was to defeat Bert.

Sue came out of the kitchen where she was making a pot of tea. She felt estranged from her father not by any wrong he had done her but by her growth in the years since he had left Torrington Street. She wondered whether her mother had said anything about what had happened in the front room. Christopher stood in the narrow passage-way, looking at her. She was a girl with long-boned hands and feet, with a body of the same pattern, and with the firm flesh she should

59

have. It seemed to her father understandable that she should have been taken, and not very monstrous. Until this moment he had thought she was a child.

"I'm going to be married, Dad." Sue no longer seemed embarrassed. The delivery of her own news made it unnecessary to expend any care on the adjustment of her relationship with her father.

The mind of Christopher Homm was filled with the consciousness of complete defeat. His daughter's marriage was settled and he was not needed. Already Felicia was tramping slowly up the stairs, taking her hat off, as on one of the ordinary days of years before. At the top, however, she turned and looked down on her victim:

"You hang up your coat on that peg." It was a generous permission.

In the dining room, Susan unobtrusively set a third place for tea. The cup she gave her father was cracked. Over the top of the tea-cosy, Felicia was addressing Christopher ten minutes later as if he had at last been able to return from some necessary journey reluctantly undertaken.

"I expect it's nice to be back, isn't it?"

It wasn't bad. When tea was over Susan cleared away and her father let himself down into the arm-chair by the fire.

So astonished was Felicia at the success of her enterprise that it was some weeks before she recovered her full malice.

VIII

ALTHOUGH FELICIA HARDLY NOTICED IT THE DAY she brought him back to Torrington Street, Christopher Homm had aged considerably during his absence. When he returned, it was to begin the epoch which ended in his senility and finally death. The period of his desertion was supposed to have been given over to the more ordinary depravities, but at any rate during the latter part of it this was far from having been the case.

The house in which he had had his room was not entirely respectable, but it was inhabited for the most part by people so old and tired that they might have been taken for virtuous. The principal tenant was a woman who had set up as a widow. She played the rôle of landlady to three other inhabitants besides Christopher Homm. Only one of these persons still engaged in activities of a kind officially recognized as vicious. This was Mrs Semelee, a woman of forty-five who from time to time left her room empty for a night, for a week or for a day or two.

Christopher Homm could not help eyeing Mrs Semelee as she went in and out. It was her body, which was plump and friendly, that he looked at, rather than her face which was set in the hardness of covetousness and fear. He was, moreover, less conscious of looking at her than of averting his eyes. For with his failing strength had come a resolve to live free of such enticements.

The interior of Homm's room did not look like the reflection of great indulgences. It was a dirty room, but it had not the squalor which is the symbol of a weakness persistently yielded to. Its disorder was merely provisional and betokened a resolution to order often deferred, not any abandonment to disorder. Its diet was of a slow ingraining that had entered carpets and chair-covers. Christopher Homm had struggled, it was evident, to prevent a complete obloquy.

On one side of the empty fireplace stood a broken-springed arm-chair wrapped in a loose cover which had often been smoothed but never mended or ironed. Beside it, on the hearth, was a gas-ring on which the rust was partly covered by shiny and sticky films of the stews and liquids that had boiled over on it, and the tiles of the hearth were stained and spotted by the same substances. The rug before the fireplace had a pattern of orange roses which was darkening into the general gloom of the chamber. Against the wall opposite was a divan bed, made as neatly as the torn and bedraggled counterpane allowed of. The table was covered with a cloth of almost edible thickness but of a poisonous and shiny green peculiar to hired rooms, and black stains had here and there superseded the dusty pile. On the shelves of the open cupboard beside the chimney piece could be seen chipped white plates under the cracked glaze of which sprawled healthless flowers belonging to an unnature that did not know grass.

It was from this sour spot that Christopher Homm set out each morning to his work at the warehouse. His body was carefully prepared, not by much washing but by a patient smoothing and drawing on of clothes, by a scraping of his cheeks and, when he was almost fully dressed, a freshening of the tired skin of his brow and neck with a damp cold flannel. At the last moment before his departure he drank a mug of tea and ate a bit of bread and cold bacon.

For Christopher Homm there was no misery in these asceticisms. He was almost happy at the regular unfolding of his simple life. Nothing disturbed him except the occasional woes of his own spirit, which the emptiness of his days enabled him to relish as it enabled him to relish his joys.

When he came back in the evening it was to the same simplicities as he had left in the morning. He would hang his raincoat up behind the door and kneel on the hearth-rug to prepare himself a pot of tea. Only when he had drunk this would he fetch from his raincoat pocket whatever morsel he had bought for himself in the course of the day. The lining of the raincoat pocket which was his daily larder was stained with the blood of the chops he occasionally bought; it was dusty with the earth that potatoes and carrots had brought with them from a world where things grew. In the bottom of the pocket were crumbs of the two or three little cakes it was his custom to buy for the weekend.

For meat Christopher Homm took whatever the butcher gave him, but whatever the cut it found its way, when the newspaper had been peeled off it, into the saucepan in which he made his stews. A few bits of vegetable followed it, and a pinch of salt, and then it was only a matter of patience until a passable meal was ready. Homm spent the interval poring over the newspaper and occasionally prodding the contents of his stewpot with a fork or a knife. He relished these moments of waiting and prodding more than he did the stew, and it was often with a sigh of reluctance that he decided that the time had come to get down the flower-patterned plate from the cupboard and to pour on to it the contents of the saucepan.

Despite the isolation he lived in Christopher Homm was not without moral and even domestic preoccupations. Instead of the care of physical persons, so active and so obtrusive, he had only to order so many passive tokens in the form of notes and coins. He had reduced his remaining humanity almost to a supersensible world of mathematics. At the end of the week he would lay out his earnings on the table. They did not vary, but none the less he felt each week that he was faced with fresh problems in their distribution.

He began with himself, with whom he found it a pleasure to be frugal. On the margin or the empty stop-press of a newspaper he would scratch with a stump of pencil all that he would need to get for himself, meat, bread, milk, potatoes, and carrots and the other provisions it was his habit to buy. The seasonal variations in the price of vegetables, which he studied with care, added an element of variation and uncertainty to this part of the calculation. The sudden if rare intrusion of an unusual expense such as the purchase of a cheap shirt or a pair of socks, set problems over which he would brood for hours. It was not, however, that Christopher Homm's earnings were not fully adequate to his modest way of life. It was partly that he was saving. Each week he took a small sum to the Post Office and it was one of his esotericisms to watch with an inner satisfaction the mounting of this total. The greatest single expenditure each week was, however, the sum which, in spite of his desertion, he sent each week to Felicia at 92 Torrington Street. The determination of this sum was a matter on which he expended his utmost powers of thought. It involved sometimes even the manipulation of his capital funds. If in the same week he resolved to send Felicia a largish sum and found that he himself needed to buy a pair of shoes, it was a major event. He could then go with a self-torturing pleasure and withdraw some money from the Post Office. When the book came back to him with the sum entered he gazed on it with the proud feelings of one who had made an enormous sacrifice.

The determination of the sum to be sent to Felicia was a mode of his fantasy. He never wrote a line when he sent the money, and never indicated an address, so that he could have no word from Felicia. She would have come to see him or at least have sent him long argumentative letters. But out of what he regarded dimly as a sense of duty he thought long each week about what Sue's and Felicia's needs would be.

They must be kept respectable. Felicia each week opened with a greedy hand the envelope he sent and remarked impatiently to Sue what a fool her father was not to send a regular sum so that she would know where she was.

"One day he'll send us nothing and then where shall we be?"

So would she declaim, though she did not in her heart believe that Christopher would leave them penniless while he had something to send. But she could hardly have guessed that, in a week when she received a large sum, it was because her husband had decided that she needed a new body-belt and had carefully priced a suitable article by gazing in the window of each of the draper's shops in the High Street. Sometimes Christopher Homm would run his hand through his hair and deplore that Sue was wearing her shoes out so fast that she must certainly have some more before she started school again.

Sometimes in the evening when his cooking was done, and always on Sundays, which were too empty even for him, Christopher Homm would go for long indeterminate walks about the streets. If on these journeys he came across any place where a crowd was gathering he would edge up and join it. It was less curiosity than a need for dumb and unobtrusive society which could be satisfied by a crowd around a bargain sale or a political meeting.

But Christopher Homm was not without his curiosity nor without his involvements in the great world of affairs. When he came up to the edge of a political meeting he looked with a trace even of anxiety to see whether he knew the speaker and whether any of his old comrades might be among the bystanders. For Christopher Homm had left off politics. He had done so gradually, almost unobtrusively, taking less and less part until he took none, and he did not wish the peace he had found to suffer the irruption of an enthusiast.

But he would stand with pleasure within hearing of an orator who did not know his history. He would stand on the edge of the crowd, and if the discourse were long he would find himself at the end immediately below the front of the portable platform. Most of the original audience would have gone and he would be encircled by newcomers.

What Christopher Homm hoped to hear more about on these occasions was Justice. It was rather as if he were eavesdropping with the design of hearing, from those who now kept company with her, the doings of one who had formerly been his mistress. But the relations of Christopher Homm with Justice had never been improperly intimate. She had merely been a reigning beauty whose toast he had drunk and whose name he had invoked. And her relations with the speakers he now listened to seemed to be of the same abstract kind.

A commonplace little man with a wide mouth would stand on the dais thumping and spitting over some recital of cumbrous fact. To this Christopher Homm listened as to a prelude or introduction the interest of which was only in the grand question or assertion to which it led. He listened subduedly, with no flicker on his face or exultation in his spine to answer the emphasis and feigned enthusiasm of the speaker. It was when the speaker at last paused that the flesh of Christopher Homm became tremulous with hope. Often the speaker would start a further recital of facts, and Homm would sink back into his apathetic but persistent attention. Sometimes, however, the point would be followed by:

"Do you call that Justice? Is that Justice for you?"

These allusions to his supreme mistress thrilled the heart of Christopher Homm. He could appreciate, too, the embittered allusions that were sometimes made to her elusiveness.

"There isn't any justice for the working man. There is no such thing. It's a word the bosses use when they want to kid you. Never believe them."

Christopher Homm understood such assertions as stating merely that this arch lady was not to be had at every street corner. The notion that by a theory of history she could be whisked altogether out of time and that any eternity into which she might flee could by the same instrument be destroyed would have been unintelligible to him. He rather liked to hear her elusiveness proclaimed because that added to the distinction of his own slight connexion with her. Moreover, when he heard allusions to this one of her characteristics which he knew so well he felt that he shared with the orator a secret of high life.

If the oratory of political enthusiasts stirred in Christopher Homm memories of a past which now seemed remote, there were other salvationists who made him uneasy about his future. Wandering through the streets he would hear, sometimes far off, the drums and trombones of that army, and he felt like a stag who hears the huntsman call. At first he would shy away but, whether through the care of an inescapable providence or because he was fascinated by his fear, more often than not he would find himself, a few minutes afterwards, face to face with these determined men and their silvery instruments. The red on their caps and collar-bands glowed like hell-fire, and Christopher Homm was not sure whether these encased men were a phalanx from darkness or mere emissaries of a world of light. When, caught in their music, he was inclining for a moment to the latter view, one of the men would open his mouth and emit such threats that Christopher Homm saw all hell smoking around him.

And yet this Zoroastrian world was hardly real to Christopher Homm. His anxiety was a fear that he had not

67

properly apprehended the reality which lay beyond the torments of the world, and this unending battle of black and white seemed to him more like a Punch and Judy show of menacing proportions than anything that could be an answer to his questions. When he had listened to the Salvationists for a little while he would turn away.

Christopher Homm had reformed himself rather than been saved. The gradual dying of his heat, and occasional weaknesses and pains that warned him that his body was moving now towards its dissolution, turned itself into a narrowing prudence. This had become his rule of conduct. It was on such a principle that he now hurried past the girls who looked too hard at him in the street, and averted his eyes from Mrs Semelee when they sought to caress her rotundities. He had almost abandoned liquor because the contrast between its temporary exhilaration and his habitual apathy made him too clearly aware of the nullity of his ordinary condition. In such retractions there was hardly room for a vivid repentance.

IX

CHRISTOPHER HOMM'S ENCOUNTER WITH MRS SEMELEE had been the type of all the sins of lust that had bemused him in his isolated life. Coming one night from the warehouse at an hour when night was beginning to drop its tentacles over the streets and it was still uncertain whether the streets would have the resolution to light up all their lamps to resist, he saw Mrs Semelee standing in a doorway. The shop had just closed, and the hanging clusters of papers and books had been taken inside. Behind the glass there were the yellow westerns, across the covers of which cowboys rode waving their guns, and stories of crimes which began with a red-lipped girl on her back, with her dress torn from one breast so as to set in alabaster the blood that trickled from it. Christopher Homm could stop without confessing to himself that it was not this desperate cowboy, or this slim victim of crime, that he was to gaze upon, but the solid meats offered by the woman in the doorway. He turned his face towards the books and his eyes wandered surreptitiously to the right to where Mrs Semelee stood. It was her calves that he could most easily look on, and they were finely cut and promised to be both soft and firm to the hold. Mrs Semelee had seen to it when she dressed that an attentive watcher could have no doubt that her thighs were of the same pattern and substance. Slowly Christopher Homm raised his eyes, and when his gaze had rested awhile between her breasts he lifted it until he was looking into her smiling face. Mrs Semelee, for all the greed and squalor which had hardened and chilled her eyes, had a physical kindness she could not, even in the pursuit of commerce, entirely put off. Her virtues as well as her vices were built into her body. Christopher Homm could not withstand even the possibility of a kindness. He drew near to Mrs Semelee without having formed an intention and she, who was not forgetful of her purposes, turned to give him her arm.

"Well, love," she said.

Christopher Homm put his fingers gingerly upon the plump bare arm, and from that moment he was truly captive. The couple began to walk along the pavement. Although it was at the instigation of the most trivial lust that Christopher Homm had stopped near where Mrs Semelee stood, now he was with her he felt a need for society. He was therefore in no hurry to proceed to the business of the evening.

"What about a drink?" he said.

They went into the saloon bar of the Dragon and Garter and Christopher ordered a pint of mild for himself and something more expensive for Mrs Semelee. The two of them looked like an old married couple as they sat at the little table sipping their drinks as if they had been talking over the faults and aspirations of a growing family. Christopher Homm even thought for a moment that it would have been all right with Felicia if she hadn't been so starched about going into pubs. But it was neither so easy to make conversation, nor to sit silently, with a woman he had just picked up off the streets as it would have been with a seasoned spouse.

"I like a drop of beer after a day's work," he said at last.

Mrs Semelee's theory was that he was some harassed and generally virtuous husband who had for one evening thrown his wife and prudence to the winds. She framed her remarks to encourage such a one.

"Well, why shouldn't you have a drop?" she said. "Nothing wrong with it that I can see. Why shouldn't a man have a bit of comfort?"

The real comfort was Mrs Semelee herself. She was at once issuing a further invitation and preaching a doctrine of her own innocence. Christopher Homm enjoyed this moment when he had before him all he wanted in the world; his pleasure was in the contrast this luxury made with the struggle and narrow circumstances of the life he had led. He was so lordly as to offer Mrs Semelee another drink, which she accepted, and to buy another pint for himself.

The conversation continued for a while in generalities. Christopher Homm was so much a philosopher, if a silent one, that he induced people around him to cast their reflections into the form of general propositions.

"A woman likes a chap to have a bit of cheek," said Mrs Semelee.

Her companion sighed because the form of the proposition did not conceal from him that Mrs Semelee was really speaking of particulars. This infuriating trick of feminine rhetoric, which disguises the wish as a statement, was well known to him, but he found it easier to tolerate in a stranger than in Felicia, more particularly since Mrs Semelee's wish, though a little over-hasty, accorded with his own as – it was his impression – his wife's rarely did.

"So you wouldn't mind a bit of cheek from me," said Christopher Homm with a sort of deductive gallantry.

Mrs Semelee banged her thigh against his to indicate that he had drawn the appropriate conclusion. She did not want to be too long in making sure that her customer meant business.

At this time Mrs Semelee had a room in the basement of a straight-fronted house in what must once have been a genteel street. It was to this that she led her victim. As they descended the steps into the area Christopher Homm thought of himself as entering, not the pit of hell, but a bear-pit in which he was soon to be at clutches with the animal. It was in this character that he saw Mrs Semelee as she unlocked the door and shuffled in. On the right of the narrow passage was a door which led into the theatre. Here was a divan bed, made up with the disguises of a typist's bed-sitting room, and a gas ring like Christopher Homm's own but cleaner. A dust-laden last light fell steeply upon the scene from the pavement above.

Mrs Semelee put on the light and drew the curtains. Then she playfully kissed her Christopher who, though he had expected this seal of their temporary compact, had the drooping manner of one helplessly astonished. His bear or Circe then decided, with the neatness of a doctor selecting one of a few familiar drugs, that this was a case for creating an illusion of domesticity rather than of any excessive passion. She had revised her theory that she had to do with a husband escaped for the night: she now inclined to the view that she had to do with a man unmarried and lonely.

"It's out there if you want to know where it is." She was kindly remembering her guest's two pints of beer. In the sordid gloom of a rarely cleaned lavatory Christopher eased himself of the liquid encumbrance and returned to find Mrs Semelee kneeling beside a kettle on the gas-ring.

"What about a cup of tea before we begin anything?"

The two passed the time while the kettle was boiling in sober and virtuous conversation. The weather of the day can still be a topic to a man on the verge of adultery. It was agreed which of the five descriptions known to them should be applied to the weather, and this done, Mrs Semelee made the tea.

It would have been dangerous as well as inconvenient to attempt any amorous encounter while both protagonists were holding cups of scalding tea; nor could they safely put them down on the divan unless they continued to sit as quietly as a pair of conversation mice. The spectacle they presented, while their tea was cooling, was therefore of an ageing widower about to make the most solemn proposals to a buxom lady some years his junior. Mrs Semelee herself found the situation not without relish; it gave her a temporary and by no means unwelcome respectability. For Mr Homm, the delay was pleasant because he knew he could end it when he chose and because, being a philosopher, he preferred inaction before all things.

It was his hostess who arose and took away his cup, the clinking of which, as she put it down, was like a bugle calling to action. He arose too, and embraced Mrs Semelee as she turned towards him.

Nothing more rapidly chases away the philosophic spirit than a touch of the flesh, and the instant he pressed this meaty person in his arms Christopher Homm lost his distaste for action. When she perceived that she was about to be undressed, Mrs Semelee disengaged herself a moment to light the gas-fire. The little delays she made the fingers of her chamberman encounter were designed less to heat his passion than to give the gas-fire a chance of taking the chill off the room. Mrs Semelee's garments were of the simplest, so that it needed some ingenuity to delay the undressing. But she saw to it that the hook of her brassière caught in her vest, and that her suspenders had need to be persuaded. When at last she stood naked before him her body was not a disappointment to him. There was immensely more of her than there was of him, and her surface was smooth, not distended but filled like a skinful of water. Christopher Homm's hands caressed her with approval from shoulder to thigh.

This Eve did not look a person readily mutable. She was marmoreal in the purposely shaded light. The soles of her muscular feet could have carried her without shame into a world of sunlight. Or she could, in a labouring world, have trodden a winepress. But it was to neither of these possibilities that she had been called. Christopher Homm drew her to the shabby bed.

She put herself between the sheets for warmth, and Christopher Homm began his own undressing. Very carefully he took off his jacket and waistcoat and hung them up behind the door. Then he took off his collar and tie and put them down beside the tea things. His braces threatened for a moment to be as difficult as Mrs Semelee's suspenders. It was no reluctance of his that made them behave so, but now he was trembling a little in anticipation of coming to grips with his beauty. At last he managed what he wanted to do, stepped out of his trousers and folded them over the back of a chair. A noble figure he looked, with his shirt tails hanging and his socks still half way up his calves. He acquired a further grotesqueness as he struggled to pull his shirt over his head, exposing as he did so what would have been better hidden. But the completed figure, when the struggle was finished, had all the joints and hollows of a body that Rodin might have made into metal. If there was any indignity about it, it was in the hopeless drooping of the mouth and the bobbing of the Adam's apple as Homm swallowed again and again the nothing in his throat.

He got into bed and lay beside Mrs Semelee, only moving a hand now and again as if to take his bearings. Mrs Semelee put out the light by a switch she could not reach without showing a bare shoulder and breast for a moment above the surface of the clothes, and an arm that might have been reaching for Excalibur. Just as Christopher Homm was settling to his task in the dark there was a rattle and a knock at the basement door. Mrs Semelee's improbable explanation as she climbed out of bed to answer it was that it must be the gas man. She folded over her bare skin an old dressing gown of soiled towelling and pushed her feet into slippers before she left the room. Christopher Homm heard the murmur of a discussion that seemed to him long. The thought that the visitor might be a husband or some other inconvenient person crossed his mind but made no impression on it. He was conscious only of the interruption of his pleasure, and of his desire for its resumption.

Mrs Semelee came back and her body was as soft and cool as flour as she put herself once more beside him.

"It's a funny time for the gas man to call," she said. "I wonder why he had to come at that time."

Mrs Semelee had no right to complain. Christopher Homm did not think he was hearing words designed to convey the truth; he said nothing, and resumed his self-imposed duty as one might an interrupted meal. In his pleasure he had the illusion that he was receiving affection. It would have surprised him if he could have seen the bored irritated look Mrs Semelee was wearing under cover of the dark. It would have surprised him if he could have seen his own greedy, slobbering lips.

Christopher Homm stayed the whole night because there was no reason why he should not. When he awoke he was feeling so domesticated that he began to think of taking breakfast with Mrs Semelee. She, however, was preoccupied and took it for granted that he would be off at once. Her flesh was commonplace in the daylight and there were faults in it, even symptoms of advancing age. She hurriedly put on her clothes and it was in the figure of a slovenly charwoman that she let him out.

On several occasions in the following year or two, Christopher Homm encountered Mrs Semelee and he became so accustomed to what seemed to him to be the chance of it that he was not surprised when he found she had taken a room in the same house as himself. But by this time he had grown chaste and withdrawn and since her arrival he had, when he was rescued by Felicia, done no more than follow Mrs Semelee with his glances.

X

IT WAS A CHARACTERISTIC OF CHRISTOPHER HOMM'S encounters of love that he sought in them little imitations of monogamy. He sought companionship also in cups. Wandering in streets in which he felt himself to be alone, it was pleasant to know that he could turn into any one of several public houses and so unite himself with a little company of those who accepted him as a familiar. In one or two places they even knew his name. In several more they knew what his drink was and smilingly produced it without his asking. It was as if his slippers had been put out for him when he came home at night.

"I don't need to ask you what it's to be, Mr Homm."

There was a quality of insulation about Christopher Homm which prevented barmen and barmaids addressing him in any more familiar form. He would nod and enjoy this little respectability.

He liked best to settle on a stool near the bar and he always inspected his beer carefully before he drank it. He would hold it up to the level of his eyes and stare at it as if he were a madman or an expert. But he never made any comment except a grunt if a barman asked him if it was all right.

"All right, Mr Homm?"

"U u u u h!"

That was supposed to mean at any rate toleration. It was remarkable to see how, after this hesitant beginning, when he lifted his pint a second time it was to swallow it almost in one long pouring. The drink was taken like a remedy for one who had been dehydrated. Thus watered, Christopher Homm opened his sticky eyelids and began to look around him.

"Same again, Mr Homm?"

Christopher Homm treated this with disdain. It was a thing to be taken for granted that he would want a second pint. This was the one with which his positive enjoyment began. After drinking a quarter of it he looked round for someone to talk to. If there were no-one else idle and alone, the barman would by instinct draw near him.

"Just out for a bit of a walk round like, Mr Homm?"

"I might be," Christopher would reply. On one of his peripatetic evenings such a question would evoke at once the long intersecting streets along which he could pick the tortuous route that would satisfy his fantasy.

"You must wear out some shoe-leather."

This might be either a compliment or a taunt. Christopher Homm was content to leave it in that ambiguity. His long and restless walks were known to all the barmen in the various pubs he would call at in the course of them. Was he a healthy man, taking these journeys out of a sort of physical virtue even through so unprepossessing a terrain, a sort of urban hiker, or was he a broken-down fellow impelled to them by a touch of madness? At the Dragon and Garter the barman was a little Irishman too near himself to madness and religion to wonder at what was nearly miraculous in his customer. The fumes of the stale bar and the aroma of peat from his remote bog were alike friendly to a stupidity that allowed play to his deepest instincts. In this man's company Christopher Homm felt comforted. It was as if he had the silent company of beasts, of the horse who clops deliciously and expectedly as you push him over from one side to the other of his stall; of the cow lowing softly as you feel for her udders. It was at the bar of the Crown that Christopher Homm felt less easy about the enquiries that were made of him. There a cockney and clever man winked at another customer as he drew Homm's beer. Here jests were made that felt to Homm in his more maudlin moods bitter and disrespectful.

"On the old London to Brighton again, are you?"

"I might have a bit of a walk," Homm would say, replying as if to a remark that had been made courteously. As quickly as possible he would protect himself by taking another pint. When he had had enough he felt himself in a pit from which he could look up benignly enough to the little barman peeping over the edge. Sometimes in the depths he could gather strength enough to surge up and patronize.

"Sonny," he would say – but never before the fourth or fifth drink of the evening – "You want to get a bit of healthy exercise yourself. You wouldn't be such a spindly little devil if you did."

This could call up a laugh against the barman, who was smart and sallow like a creature the sun had never played on. It was a triumph for Christopher if someone on his side of the bar laughed humanely and said "You ast for it you know" and the barman looked sheepish. When such a triumph came to him, Christopher took another pint out of magnanimity before he moved on. Then he felt like a hero till he closed the door and found himself in the street.

The street appeared like a hope and a problem. Certainly he had no difficulty, with the amount he had taken, in following its straight course on the pavement or in the road-way, as he chose. If it were empty he would do now one and now the other, in turn, to show that he had this choice. But, no matter how familiar the route had become, it seemed to him always that he might arrive at some new place, and that the secret of this hope lay in swerving to right or to left at the fortunate intersection. He made a point of not choosing these intersections by reason. He would hurry on, and allow some sudden tropism to turn him at the appropriate corner. In this way he could at any rate sometimes be lost, and that was a happiness. If there were a great obscurity, and shadows fell upon him from all sides, he could feel himself at the bottom of the sea and run like a crab from refuge to refuge. A tree plunging upwards into the blackness would be a great weed swaying. Sudden headlights would be an octopus approaching him. In this marine world he could not lose his cares, but he could press so close to the sandy floor that it seemed to him that he might escape the consequences that threatened him. And then, from so humble a depth, he would come up suddenly when he found himself confronted by another familiar pub. It might be the Thistle.

At the Thistle everything was of a female leniency and sweetness. A lady held sway there whom none might touch but whom all might admire. Her benign countenance recognized a universal need which she soothed by so unquestionably refusing to satisfy. Her breasts and belly, the buttocks exhibited by the mirror behind her, were of a hugeness which excluded the possibility of their being real. The thin shiny dress that all but followed their contours was the uttermost frontier of the world. No man dreamed of going beyond it. Christopher Homm would lean against the bar thinking of these veiled breasts as if they were the pillars of Hercules. To one who had travelled so far nothing could be better than to know that he had come up against a boundary.

"It would be nice to be at the sea-side," the barmaid would say when he had come in from a blind night of rain, closing the door quickly lest a gust should sweep the glasses off the counter. "On a nice summer evening, I mean, with the tide coming in. I would paddle," she would go on dreamily, and Homm saw her mountainous toes like headlands with the surf breaking about them. "Then I would just sit there and do nothing. Wouldn't it be lovely?"

She laughed to break any spell she might have laid on her customers and so enable them to order again. When they had

79

done so, it was not long before she was smiling again, but at nobody, and saying perhaps:

"Or I've often thought I wouldn't mind a circus. You know, a caravan . . ." and she would build up the picture till its absurdity became apparent to her and it was time for another round of drinks.

Sometimes Christopher Homm would so far succumb to these charms as to stay until closing time, and then he went back to his lodgings in a quietness that passed without difficulty into sleep. But sometimes an intruder, not respectful of the magic of the Thistle, would break in. He would mistake the barmaid's reveries for an invitation to some obscenity of speech, or would start an argument. On such nights Christopher Homm would plunge once more into the sea outside in the hope of finding a more peaceful refuge.

He would not find it, however. Once the pillars of Hercules had failed to hold his charmed eyes he was drawn towards a nightmare of isolation. By now the liquor he had in him was enough to affect him with a kind of blindness, or rather a numbness of sense in which he saw the houses towering above him, the traffic hurtling past or people folded as far as they could be into their clothes, but none of these things had more than the most superficial visual meaning. In this state his own agonies could well out of him and compel the shapes of reality to serve him. He was a sorcerer, but his great power brought him no happiness for his very power over these images meant that he was alone.

He walked like a sober man in spite of his evil enchantment. He was not of those who fall ignominiously in the gutter but of the prouder race who, in their drunkenness, work towards some gesture of unaccustomed nobility. What grandeur Christopher Homm had was of the purest inspiration, for no plot or plan could form in that laden mind.

The only indication Christopher Homm gave of the hero

he now was was an occasional swish of the arm which was the gesture of a man who, had he been capable of forming words, would have formed noble ones. A careful observer might have seen also a subdued fury in his step, but he would not have attributed that to heroism. When Christopher Homm reached the Acorn he was drunk.

There was good reason why he should not reach that Acorn except in that condition. This pub was at the bottom of Torrington Street, and when he was sober decency and prudence alike kept him from it. It was the pub next to the chapel.

"Not that the chapel people use it much," he might reflect if he suffered an interval of reason.

Christopher Homm opened the door of the Acorn with such violence that everyone standing at the bar looked round at him.

"Why it's Mr Homm. Good evening to you," the barman would say.

The customers at the bar shuffled to make space for this inspired man to order his drink.

"You can make it a pint and put some gin in it." When he had reached this state Christopher Homm was determined to reach the furthest recesses of the caverns opening before him.

"You still living up Torrington Street?" the barman said to him one evening.

Christopher Homm looked at him as if he would smash the beer mug against his teeth, and then a drunkard's prudence came to him and he smiled kindly:

"Still up there," he said, without saying who was. And then: "The missis and kid mostly." It was vague, but the impression that he gave was that he too belonged there.

The barman would not venture on such a discourtesy but a customer who knew more about Homm than the rest of them taunted him:

"You better go and see them next door now. Go and give 'em a 'ymn."

Christopher Homm dripped and drivelled into his beer. He grumbled blasphemies and indecencies until the landlord came over to him and said:

"Hi, go a bit steady now old chap. We don't want no trouble in here."

To show he was not afraid Homm went on with his swearing as if it were a task he had to finish. But he swore more quietly until, as if fearing that someone might think him subdued, he banged his mug on the bar and said he would go and see what they was up to next door.

They was not up to anything. They was not there at all. If there had been a meeting that night the faithful had already scattered to their pious homes. Christopher Homm thundered with his forearms on the dark green painted door.

"I'll teach the bastards to keep me out," he shouted.

Only the slow hammer of a policeman's hooves approaching along Torrington Street prevented the accomplishment of the design Homm was already forming of tearing down the texts from the noticeboard beside the door.

The policeman came towards him as if he were approaching prey.

"What you making that row hammering for? Get along quietly."

The attitude Christopher Homm at once adopted was so genteel that the policeman began to doubt whether he had really to do with a drunk.

"They seem to have gone home," said Homm. "Ah, I see the light's out."

The policeman could not badger so reasonable a wayfarer. Like a chapel-goer, Christopher Homm made his way along Torrington Street. In No. 92 there were lights on upstairs. Felicia would be doing up her hair for the night. The kid would be asleep in the back room. Christopher had a key and he was tempted to use it. He would go upstairs and pull Felicia's hair while she still had it about her shoulders.

This however was a movement of the mind not of the body. Christopher Homm did not venture an inch from the gatepost he was still holding. He even feared to move lest the sound of what he did should be heard within. He imagined the curtain drawn back, and Felicia there with her white nightgown and loose hair, holding in one hand a brush that was a sceptre of justice. He knew that if that happened he could not have stirred while the avengeress descended the stairs. The door would open and become light; he put his hands above his head to protect himself from the blows of the brush that he knew must fall upon it. In this apprehension he stood until the light in Felicia's room went peacefully out and he slid forward like a man in a wood whom a prowling panther had unexpectedly ignored. The journey back to his own place of concealment was undertaken as if he were an object of pursuit; he who, in fact, the world could utterly dispense with.

XI

NO MORE SOLID REASON HAD DRIVEN CHRISTOPHER
Homm away from Torrington Street than, on nights of
drunkenness, occasionally brought him back to look at his
own front door. There had been a week, much like any other,
in which Felicia cajoled and raged against him, and he
showed his teeth like a rat in a corner. On Sunday evening
Felicia came home from chapel, which had been cold, to
find her husband comfortable. This was an offence. Christopher Homm was not only comfortable but he had enjoyed
his wife's absence. Opened newspapers and full ashtrays
showed what kind of a debauch he had enjoyed. On Monday
Felicia let Christopher get his own breakfast. When he came
back from work, she at once set him to work mending Susan's
shoes. When that was done and Christopher hoped for
supper, Felicia was deep in some other task and looked
injured when he suggested eating. On Tuesday Christopher
came home, spread his newspaper on the table, and shouted
to Felicia that he would have his supper right away. On
Wednesday evening Felicia went out. On Thursday Christopher did not come home until the Acorn closed, and when
he came he was a mighty man who threw Felicia's things
from the bedside chair on to the floor to make room for his
own. Felicia kept the light on for three hours so that she could
observe, on her husband's weary face that was pretending
sleep, the ravages of her incessant scolding. On Friday
Felicia watched every mouthful Christopher ate at breakfast
and left her own plate empty until he had gone. For the
evening she arranged the inconvenience of several female
visitors. A plate of cold was put in the kitchen for Christopher

while the ladies gossiped and cut out all over the dining room table. When at last the visitors had gone Felicia spoke for an hour on she supposed she was never to be allowed to do anything. After dinner on Saturday Christopher was sent to do shopping in the High Street. He came back sullenly with the wrong purchases. He was sent out again, and it was from this expedition that he did not return.

Christopher had placed his shopping basket carefully on the fishmonger's counter. He intended to leave it there, like a man on a parade-ground flinging down his equipment and declaring that he would soldier no more. Then it occurred to him that it was a pity to waste the mackerel. He therefore extracted the pair of them, naked, and put them in the pocket of his raincoat. In a moment of lucidity he smiled to think how Felicia would regard this outrage. But he ceased to smile when, as he began to walk along the pavement, he saw her coming to meet him. Felicia, like a mother descending on guilty children, could see at once what was wrong with him.

"What have you done with that shopping bag?" were her first words.

Christopher felt a pleasurable anger.

"Chucked it away," he said, and waited to see the effect of his words.

Felicia could not credit this indiscipline.

"Don't be a fool," she said. "Where is it?"

Christopher repeated that he had chucked it away.

"You can go and get it," he added, "if you want it. It's on the counter."

Felicia could not understand what had happened, but her prudence was stronger than her desire to know. She therefore began to move towards the fishmonger's, intending to recover the basket before she interrogated her husband.

Christopher did not want his anger to be disappointed.

There it was like a dumpling at his heart, cooking gently. It would be a waste not to discharge it and to spread ruin around him. He turned to follow Felicia, who was already coming back with the shopping basket in a half-extended hand.

"It's empty," she said. "If you haven't bought the fish where's the money?"

"Oh, I bought them all right," said Christopher with an almost rustic chuckle. "Too late to get your money back now."

Felicia became taut with exasperation. It was as if the string in her vertebrae were being drawn tight.

"I gave you half-a-crown, where is it? You're not having that for beer money." She raged at the thought that her husband might be winning an advantage. "If there's going to be any treats it's about Sue's and my turn." When Christopher did not reply Felicia added. "Well, you won't get no supper."

Solving the puzzle of Christopher's behaviour meant little to Felicia, but it infuriated her that she was in the presence of an insubordination.

"Look sharp and give me that money," she resumed after a bit. "That's out of the housekeeping and I'm having it back."

"I give you too much housekeeping." Christopher's voice was that of a man making not a general assertion but a particular explanation and Felicia perceived this refinement. But she replied with a disquisition on the price of things.

Christopher was slowly preparing his surprise. He dared not think of it clearly himself until it was ready, and it was at the very moment that it came to his own consciousness that he said to his wife:

"I shan't be worrying you for supper. Nor breakfast. I'm going to look after myself."

86

"I'd like to see you looking after yourself," said Felicia, not seizing the gravity of his point. "Me and Sue can go out to the pictures I suppose and leave you to it?"

That was not the point at all.

"I don't mean just this evening. I'm going off on my own."

Felicia could still not credit that he meant just that. She looked at him for a moment almost with concern, as if he and not she were about to suffer.

"I'm going to clear out." Christopher had begun to grow anxious lest, failing to make his explanation clear, his enterprise itself should suddenly lose reality and he go home to Torrington Street.

He began to cast around for an action of great solemnity that would convey his meaning as words could not. He had the design of striking his wife on the face with the flat of his hand, but with lucidity he rejected that as liable to entangle him in a row in which he would lose his freedom. Then he thought of taking off his mackintosh and handing it to his wife, as one who should say: "I go from you naked and have no need of possessions." He rejected this because the meaning of it seemed to be insufficiently patent. Then he put his hands in his pocket and ran them along the cold mackerel. He pulled the pair of them out and swung them in the air before the astonished Felicia.

"That's your supper," he said, putting one of the fish close under her nose. "And this is mine." He shook his own by the tail and replaced it in his pocket.

"Go on, take it." Felicia was fond of mackerel but she did not seem in a hurry to take this one. Suddenly Christopher pulled back the front of her dress and dropped it into her bosom. There was a scandalized murmur from two or three shoppers round about and while Felicia was extracting the fish Christopher made off in the crowd.

87

Christopher's final gesture to his wife was well chosen. It succeeded in conveying to her, as words had not done, that this was a decisive and extraordinary moment of time. Moreover, the enormity of his action dazed her while he made his escape. And this escape was perhaps finally possible only because, as Christopher boarded a bus to get away as quickly as possible, the comedy of the action concealed from him implications he could not at that moment have borne.

The rest of the day Christopher spent in shielding himself from the truth of what he had done. As soon as he could he picked up an evening paper, because the unreality of the news was a protection. By allowing a murder of two girls to crawl over his mind he managed to travel several miles in the bus without being conscious of what he had done. In this he was assisted by a few words inserted by the journalist to suggest that the girls were pretty and insufficiently clothed. He was in danger of being cast back upon reality when a story of divorce took him into a world of dressing-gowns and contraceptives. With the help of an accident in which bodies had been unusually mangled he managed to get to Westminster Bridge.

Here he got off and looked at the river, from whose shining expanse was reflected something which, caught in his mind, seemed for a moment like an aspiration. He had the illusion that he was about to be free. The distant cranes evoked great ships and remote waterways. He recollected an earlier servitude which, in retrospect, had the deceptive look of a mastery. Clumsy and hopeless though he had always in fact been, it seemed to him that once he could have thrown a rope round a capstan or winkled a way over the sea with an oar. Such a man was surely right to leave Torrington Street to take his place once more in a world of loose muscles and unworrying action.

It was in this false resolution that he swung on to the embankment. He had soon to admit, however, that he was not walking towards anything and to slacken his pace. He decided that if he could not be a hero of action he could at least be a philosopher. But philosophers cannot stand idle if the wind is cold. Christopher Homm crossed the road, skirted Parliament Square, and rambled along Millbank. The towering buildings darkened his course and he came to the open and unfinished stretch that contains the Tate. He climbed the steps of the Gallery, but their magnificence left him feeling exposed as a naked statue on a pedestal. When he turned round to look at the river again it was not with aspiration but in loneliness. The unemployed spaces seemed too vast for one who had shrivelled for protection behind the heavily curtained windows of Torrington Street or between the rows of boxes in a shoe warehouse. Moreover, Homm did not feel secure in the company that dawdled on the steps. There were one or two ladies expensively dressed, and several people, men and women, as seedily attired as he was himself but who appeared to be so by outrance and deliberation, which is a different sort of poverty.

Christopher Homm knew that the gallery housed pictures and statues. He had come up the steps without any formed plan of cultivating his mind, but now that he felt lonely he thought of Felicia again and began to tell himself that he would have time for such matters now he was free. This was an ambition so long buried as to be meaningless to him. He had the sense not to put it to any test by entering the gallery. Instead, he made an effort to enjoy a reverie of future cultivation. The effort did not come to much, and he soon abandoned it for the reflection that the gallery was closing. That was a solid reason for doing nothing that day.

Slowly he descended the steps and went in search of other forms of liberty. He found them as night fell in the imperfectly washed temptations that hung about the shadows of Pimlico. Under a vast portico he discoursed with a girl who was uncertain whether he was a potential customer or a poor person to whom she could talk without any attempt to be engaging. Christopher Homm, feeling morally obliged to spend the night in a debauch whatever his natural inclination to virtue, began awkwardly to make it clear that he was a customer. Before he had quite made his point, however, he recollected that he had only thirty shillings in his pocket and that, if he were to stick to his resolution of not returning home, he could have no more till his next pay day. He therefore began to disengage from the conversation. The girl did not hinder him, for she could read purses as some read minds. It was getting late and she did not want the evening to be unprofitable.

Christopher Homm made his way back to the embankment. He was chilly and wind-worn, and he could not find even a coffee-stall at which he might warm his stomach. The late buses trundling over Westminster Bridge, when at last he reached it again, would have turned his mind to the ignoble warmth of his own house had not his pride in his new rôle forbidden any such revolution. Christopher Homm stood so long at the end of the bridge that policemen began to circle around him like crows waiting for death. He made, self-consciously and in turn, the casual and formal movements he imagined might have suggested themselves to a respectable inhabitant of a suburb who was thinking of returning, after a sober evening, to his well-found home. Then he glanced at Big Ben and turned up the collar of his raincoat. There was a question he could not by any fantasy escape: Where was he to sleep, or should he coldly wander about the streets all night? He could not decide, but just as he was slumping into a hopelessness that would have brought the police down on him, a preliminary resolution came to him and stiffened his body. One thing he must do. He walked briskly over the bridge to the middle of the river and then, approaching the rail, he took from his pocket the ceremonial mackerel and dropped it into the darkness below.

XII

THE CONDITIONS CHRISTOPHER HOMM HAD ENDED BY finding intolerable were the amenities that sensible men desire. 92 Torrington Street, although but a servile paradise, had been one. It had a good fire in winter, armchairs into which one could sink without much discomfort among the broken springs, a table with a white table-cloth on which, in the ordinary way, food presented itself at appointed intervals. It was even a place in which Christopher Homm was, on the whole, served like a master. Sue was old enough now to perform many of the operations which her father had formerly and inefficiently performed. So Felicia, wearying of his incapacity to receive instruction, had turned with zest to the more malleable material afforded by her daughter. The trouble was that the organization of these services, no less than the attempts to teach Christopher what he should do, omitted all reference to the needs of Christopher himself. It is true that he enjoyed benefits, and when Felicia told him that he did he could not deny it. But he felt these very benefits to be unaccommodating. They were not the ones he had elected, even when they were arranged specially for him. They were those which Felicia judged would do him good. When Christopher protested against some kindness Felicia could often prove that he had expressed the very desire it purported to satisfy. He had no answer, though there was one. It was that he had expressed that desire in circumstances that were quite different, at a moment when some other and quite irrelevant kindness was closing upon him. He could not explain this, because he did not understand it himself, and if he had done so he would not have dared to speak because that would have been to impugn Felicia's judgment. So he became a monster of ingratitude.

His growth in this turpitude was steady and consistent. The more his daughter grew in wisdom and household dexterity, and the more he was eased of his domestic labours, the less the kindnesses done to him touched him. He felt instead that he was the object of a desperate plot which must result in his isolation. The house worked perfectly with no further intervention from himself than the production, on Friday evenings, of a little packet of money. He was at bottom a restless man who wanted a physical reality to conform to his perceptions and it was inevitable that, in the end, he should create a world by abstracting himself from the household in which he felt he was not necessary.

There were tasks he could still perform without permission and by general command. But he had no choice in them. They were in that limited range of employments which Felicia, because she did not like them, had conceded were more suitable for a man. They did not fall within the common conception of these matters; she meant that they were more suitable for *her* man than for herself.

The first of these tasks was to make a morning pot of tea. This was more suitable for a man because the delicate Felicia did not like to leave her bed on cold mornings. Christopher must creep downstairs, for Sue was a growing girl and must not be awakened too early, and stand in the kitchen while the kettle boiled. Pitiful and scraggy he looked, with his thin hair falling over a face stupid with sorrow and sleep, even in summer when such golden light as ever fell into the house entered at the kitchen window. In the long winter which made up most of the year he would for cold pull on his trousers and a jersey before he came downstairs. At all times he stood there an unfinished man, something that the sculptor had not the heart to chip any more. When the steam blew out in clouds he left his statuesque position like one who was entering life with reluctance. He heated the teapot as a careful duty. Pouring away the water he had used for heating it he was an alchemist with the most refined of concoctions. But when he stood by Felicia's bedside with her steaming cup it was as a lady's maid not venturing to hurry or perturb a mistress awakening with an insolent slowness.

Another job Christopher Homm could do was to clean the doorstep. This was more suitable for a man because Felicia was a bit above public humiliation on her hands and knees. Moreover, a man performing these duties in Torrington Street was making a public and unaccustomed act of homage to his wife. Felicia cared no more than Christopher for domestic kindnesses done to her, but she valued any that was done publicly enough to be supposed to modify the estimation in which she was held. Christopher no longer needed to be told to do this job. It was the penance with which he started the sabbath while Felicia and Sue were still in bed. Over his clean doorstep, a little later, mother and daughter could issue to the morning service at the chapel. Had the doorstep not been done, Felicia would have felt herself to be lacking in some praise or sanctity.

There was a third duty which lay upon Christopher Homm of which his wife would say, in describing to neighbours the services performed by her husband: "I would not even attempt it." This was man's work indeed. It consisted of repairing the family shoes. The operation was a little drama in three acts. In the first, the shoes to be repaired would collect menacingly in some prominent place. When they had outstared Christopher Homm the second act began, and he went to Woolworth's to buy the necessary material in rubber or leather. In the third act he pared and hammered and polished until the shoes he was treating looked as much as possible like those that slept coyly side by side in the boxes

94

in his warehouse. In this craftmanship he could have had pleasure but a mean resentment at the imposition of the task took the place of any more agreeable feelings. The resentment was much increased on those occasions, and they became frequent, when he perceived the hand of Felicia in the marshalling of the shoes against him and still more when, growing impatient of his response, she went to Woolworth's herself and brought home the material out of kindness. This must infuriate because it meant not only that Felicia was trespassing on a duty he would in time perform, if mournfully enough, but that she was depriving her husband of a tiny debauch among the baubles and gew-gaws of the Woolworth's counter. He loved to walk among the bright and tinny articles displayed and, picking over the standardized articles there put for sale, to pretend that there was an act of discrimination in selecting from among them.

The little services that Christopher Homm performed were more than balanced, as Felicia told him often enough, by those that she and her daughter did for him. He who felt so totally omitted from the arrangements of the house was in fact the passive regulator of most of them. He might not fix the time of a particular meal or a day for washing or ironing, but these things were fixed by reference, not it is true to any fancy he had displayed, but to the needs which a study of his blind movements had revealed. The household diet was ordered to give most of what he had once eaten with the grossest delight. Against this very objectivization of his own appetites and the translation of a whim into a habit Christopher murmured in his heart and occasionally demonstrated by a movement of revulsion. The treat it was to him to have a couple of tomatoes fried to a mash with his bacon was so well known that he was baited about it by Felicia and, following her, by Susan. The sneers that his preference elicited from his dependants made the weekly presentation of this dish to him, when at last Felicia got up on Sunday mornings, less an indulgence than a reproof or a torture. Felicia, bending over the frying-pan inattentively or chattering to Sue and issuing to her all manner of petty commands, was in fact not wholly cruel and, although she liked to chide, she hoped also that the tomato-red fry might give some pleasure. She did not for a steady moment regard her subject in order to verify her hypothesis, for she preferred conclusions without verification, but she had also the hope or theory that it would be pleasant for Christopher to be thanked for cleaning the doorstep.

"The doorstep is looking very good this morning, isn't it, Sue?"

Sue, whose method of protecting herself from her parents' ill-temper was to cloak herself in a voluminous sulk, peeped out from this envelope to answer that she hadn't noticed anything special about it when she brought the milk in. Felicia was about to reprove her daughter for this inadequate appreciation of what she had been commanded to admire. She was, however, forestalled by Christopher who, moving at a slower tempo, had just had time to develop his own objection to her original remark.

"The doorstep looks the same as what it always does when I clean it. Anyone would think I never done it before. It's every bloody Sunday the same."

Felicia was now in a rage and banged the plates on the table. Susan swung her chair unnecessarily high when she lifted it to get into her place, and then lolled on it in insolent disorder. Christopher took his place carefully and glowered at the plate before him. There was no grace but, as it were, three particular prayers to the devil. Felicia was agitated and she felt she must introduce some regulation. She adopted a tone of pleading which the other two found particularly offensive.

96

"Do eat before it gets cold," she said.

By way of reply Christopher shouted.

"It's these bloody tomatoes again!"

Felicia was hurt. This was her husband's favourite breakfast, she said, and they were done exactly as he liked them.

"I'm sick of the bloody things," he said.

Felicia thought her best course was to be calm and sanctimonious.

"Don't let Sue hear you talking like that," she said.

Christopher's way of complying with this request was to resort to outrageous deeds. He picked up his plate and tossed both bacon and tomatoes on to the floor.

"It'll do for the cat," he commented in a voice so low that it was less like an address than a thought overheard.

The splendour of Christopher's rage recalled Sue to her duty. She became subdued and crumbled her bread with one hand. Then she saw an easy way to enjoy in the eyes of her mother a superior righteousness, and started methodically to eat up her breakfast.

Felicia chose this moment to let loose a few tears. She too was beyond the hope of effecting any communication by means of speech, but experience should have taught her that she would accomplish no more by squirting water out of her eyes. This performance her husband did not take as a sign of grief but of perversity. There was indeed an element of conscious effort in this weeping, and Christopher thought himself clever to perceive it. He ignored the involuntary suffering that accompanied the effort because to have recognized it would have been to admit that he was himself cruel, whereas he preferred to think of himself as an innocent attacked by tyrants. Neither husband nor wife was willing to try the effects of humility, and mildly to wipe up the mess on the floor.

Having put his breakfast where he could not eat it without humiliation, Christopher was left without occupation. He could of course have eaten bread and margarine, but that was too like a penance for a man who had cleaned the doorstep. For several seconds he sat motionless, and then began to panic lest, in his inactivity, he should sink into some sort of defeat. So he pushed back his chair from the table, and, without uttering any further word or eating a mouthful, went into the kitchen. Then taking various pieces of equipment with him, he went heavily upstairs and shut himself in his and Felicia's bedroom. He began to pull the furniture about roughly, to the alarm of his wife below and even of Susan, who was shortly sent up by her mother:

"Do go and see what your Dad is doing."

Dad, however, had foreseen this enquiry and had pushed the wardrobe against the door. All Susan could do was to knock and at last speak through the muffling thickness of wood and clothes.

"Dad, Mum says what are you doing and do come down now."

By way of reply Christopher pushed the bed across the room with a tremendous rumble. For Susan this vast physical movement was like the menace of thunder to one lost among the hills. It was as if the sky ovehead was glowering with the fury her father had exhibited.

She did not know exactly what was happening, either in her father's mind or in the bedroom, but the house was alive with evil spirits and all her primness in eating up her breakfast could not protect or purify her. When she returned to her mother it was with the feeling that there, too, was no security. Felicia was now a cauldron in which boiled strange messes.

Felicia and Susan could not go to chapel that morning because Felicia's best hat and coat were in the barricaded room and she would not go to beg for them. So she decided she would have a good clean-up downstairs. This would have the advantage that, when Christopher re-emerged, she could reasonably be supposed to be too preoccupied to pay any attention to him. Moreover, the whole of the downstairs could be made so uncomfortable that Christopher would have nowhere to sit and read the Sunday paper. Felicia worked with a fury until the place was beyond dispute uninhabitable. Then she slackened her efforts a little. It would be a mistake to tidy up too soon.

About noon there was a further moving of furniture and Christopher reappeared. When Felicia, with a duster about her head, met him, she was distressed to see that he too had the appearance of one who had been doing some work. She was thus deprived of the glory of superior laboriousness. Christopher turned and went upstairs again and Felicia followed. One of her best clean sheets had been laid over the bed and Christopher had stripped most of the paper off the walls. The bits were everywhere, mingled with the grit of crumbled plaster.

"Well!" Felicia was astonished at the outrageous good work. She walked over the room and began to pick up and shake articles of her clothing that were now grimy and not fit to be seen.

Christopher enjoyed the scandal he had created.

"You wanted the job done didn't you?" he said.

XIII

THE HOME THAT WAS THE THEATRE OF SO MUCH bliss had, before Christopher's desertion, nearly foundered, not through lack of love or patience but through lack of money. It was doubtful whether it was more a triumph or a defeat when Christopher, at first tentatively and experimentally and at length with every appearance of deliberation, or at any rate of constancy, settled into the job at the shoe warehouse. This settlement provided money for the family, and Christopher Homm felt a certain reluctant pride in being able to make this provision. On the other hand, the regular labour thus entailed meant an abandonment of his natural wilfulness, in which he was accustomed to think of his liberty and even his life as consisting. But whether Christopher Homm was in this peace a victor or one of the vanquished, Felicia certainly mounted a triumphal car which she trusted would take her to the end of her days.

It was a fear of his wife's triumph that had kept Christopher Homm so long from performing this good work. When he had so far weakened before Felicia's exhortations as to announce that he was going to get a regular job, his first course was to institute a daily visit to places where jobs he was not likely to get were advertised. He ignored disdainfully the boards which, among advertisements for apartments to let and prams for sale, occasionally announced a vacancy for a handyman. His preferred haunt was the public library. He would enter the newspaper room with a mixture of relief and malice. The relief was in part the sense of duty, if not done, at any rate theoretically on the point of execution; in part it was mere pleasure at entering so quiet a refuge from the disorderly street. The malice was in a subdued knowledge that he had no intention, that day, of doing his duty, and a feeling that he was in some sort deceiving Felicia.

When he entered the newspaper room he looked chiefly at the wooden blocks of the floor, which seemed dusty after their morning sweep by the shabby cleaner. His eyes thus directed saw also the varnished legs of the tables and chairs not so much kicked as scuffed against by a succession of shuffling feet. They saw too the frayed turn-ups of old flannel trousers and shoes that were cracked with wear and lack of polish, and occasionally the wrinkled stockings and varicose veins of middle-aged women readers. When he raised his eyes it was to gaze on people who had detached themselves more whole-heartedly than he had himself from the world of regular effort and achieved earnings. Most of the papers looked, soon after they were put there, as dog-eared as their readers.

Christopher Homm, alike in pacification of his conscience and the pursuit of his malicious pleasure, lost no time in turning to the advertisement columns. In his pointless thoroughness he did not neglect the great papers which advertise for the gentleman who organize, if they do not rule, the world. He could thus be surprised each day at the salaries offered by people who would not admit him to their lucrative rackets. After this amazement he descended to the evening papers, then to the local papers, but every time he saw an advertisement for a job he might have done he found in it some unsuitability which prevented him from applying for it.

When he found his job it was by one of those acts which look like acts of decision, but really represent the final liquescence of irresolution. After a visit to the library he was mooching home along a side street that, after a row of tiny bay windows, was walled upwards and onwards for a vast space by blank brick. Half way along this blankness was broken by green doors that opened widely enough to receive a lorry into a cobbled court-yard. It was the first time Christopher Homm had seen these doors open. And as he saw this he saw a notice chalked on a piece of cardboard torn from a shoe box.

"Man wanted for checking."

Christopher Homm did not know what this meant. It was as if this blank enclosure, having with difficulty opened its heavy jaws, could still speak with only the barest intelligibility. One understood that it had a want, but it was clear to nobody what it was. It was perhaps this imperfect expression which attracted Christopher Homm, and that he felt himself in the presence of a mind no more lucid than his own. Without hesitating a moment he strode into the yard.

Mr Wilson was looking out on it through the window of his office. He had eyes that, through his spectacles and the glass of the window, seemed like whorls or conches. Indeed as Christopher looked at him his whole face appeared an almost flat thing, either shell or lichen, growing upon the office wall. The enclosure now seemed submarine. Christopher was a fish, poisonous and phosphorescent in those tropical waters, and it was in this character that he swam towards Mr Wilson. The latter appeared at first to flatten himself further against the wall, like some primary organism protecting itself. Then his lips and eyes began to protrude as a speech grew inside him, and the instant he began to emit it he dissolved into mere humanity and the water became air.

"What do you want looking about here for?" he asked.

Christopher Homm replied as the most reputable and rational seeker might have done, with just as much demureness as would have been natural in one who, normally in regular employment, was unaccustomed to offering his labour for hire.

"I've come about that job you got," he said.

Mr Wilson came slowly out into the courtyard. For a moment it seemed as if he might contradict Christopher Homm, denying that there was any job to be had. Then he seemed to search his mind as if something of that sort had been mislaid. At last it seemed that he had found it. Even then the way was not open for a treaty. Mr Wilson's next impulse was to say that Christopher Homm was certainly not the man he wanted. But suddenly Christopher became so meek that it was impossible to allege anything against him. Mr Wilson, always ready to give way to a weakness that was indistinguishable from kindness, said he would give Homm a trial.

"But it means work," he said. He had the pomposity of all who can say such words with the implication that work is a thing that very few people can be trusted to do. Mr Wilson's round eyes were always expressing astonishment at the commonplace, and he was never so emphatic as when he was enunciating some truth so obvious that it need not have been spoken at all. He imagined that the principles lying asleep in reality would not be there unless he drew attention to them. When he did draw attention to them, it was as if he were putting bones into an animal that could not stand up without his petty constructions.

"What you got to do is check the shoes going out and coming in. If there's a mistake your numbers won't be right. That means care all the time."

The lips of Christopher Homm began to curl in a tremendous scorn of this imbecility. He was about to raise his voice and frighten the little man back to his office when he sensed that this would be a job where he was a better man than his employer. Moreover, in the corners of the workroom behind the office he saw a refuge he knew he could inhabit. So instead of shouting he asked civilly enough what the money was.

This was another subject that provoked the aggrandisement of Mr Wilson. As a preparation for replying he increased several inches in height, width and even depth. But his density decreased. Indeed it seemed for a moment that with this inflation he might topple over like a thing without weight enough to stand firm.

"Money isn't everything in a job like this," he said. "What I want to know is do you think you'd be any good?"

Christopher Homm looked at the rows of boxes in the warehouse and apprehended the many possibilities of confusion. But his reply, like Mr Wilson's question, was an expression of will and not of any faculty he might have for perceiving the truth. If Mr Wilson grew big with menace Christopher Homm in self-defence would jab him.

"It'd be just my line," he said. He had determined to get the job, and he saw that Mr Wilson was a weak man who would believe him if he talked enough. "I've had a lot of experience checking different things. Of course you might say clerical work is what I'm used to. But I don't mind a bit of fetching and carrying." Now Christopher was condescending from a great height.

Mr Wilson looked more doubtful the more Christopher Homm talked but he was, none the less, further from refusing to take him on. He was apt to be entranced by anyone who talked to him in terms of foregone conclusions.

"And I should think I might do a bit of tidying up," Christopher said, looking at several odd boxes lying in what should have been clear corridors between the stacks of shoes. "It's a bit of a danger having them things lying about but of course you won't have had time to clear them up."

This last phrase was a flattery which Mr Wilson particularly relished, and he told his wife that evening that his new employee had shown signs of remarkable intelligence. Mrs

Wilson, who knew her man, put him out of countenance by saying:

"I suppose he saw you were very busy."

That was it, but Mr Wilson had of course to say that it didn't need a lot of intelligence to see that. He had given Homm the job because it would, in the end, be an economic proposition to employ him. The final decision had been more like a rape than an engagement.

"I suppose it's a bit late to be starting now," Christopher Homm had said. "I'll come in after I've had my dinner."

When he had gone Mr Wilson sat down in his office and wondered whether, when Homm came back he would dare to refuse him admission. He even thought of getting up and closing the big double doors and standing with his ear against the inside pretending not to hear when Christopher Homm knocked. After all there was the expense. But the expense was nothing to the difficulty of going back on what now seemed the ineluctable events of the morning. The notice "Man wanted for checking" had been put up by Wilson in a moment of voluminous self-pity. Swathed in this, he had left his muddled accounts in the office and nailed his notice to the door as a public demonstration that what he had to do was more than one man could cope with. Now this gesture, that was merely dramatic, had acquired all the sobering characteristics of real life. It had consequences even for Mr Wilson's purse. This reflection served to fill the place of work until Christopher Homm came back.

Christopher was then bolder than ever, for he had been at home boasting and he had some doubt how he would be received by his employer. As an insurance against mal-success he had said to Felicia:

"Mind he's a shifty-looking bugger and you never know which way that sort will turn."

He had been so emphatic about this that Felicia could not believe that there was a job at all.

Any reality would suffer if Felicia could not believe in it. But she felt that the job might exist if she could believe, so she pursed her lips and put the dinner on the table.

Christopher could see that his remarks about Mr Wilson were taken merely as an excuse, and when he went back to the warehouse it was with the intention that events should so fall out that he would be able in the evening to reply that his employer was shifty indeed, but unable to withstand the moral force of his new employee.

"Where shall I get cracking?"

Christopher sounded like a man accustomed to work and keen on it. Mr Wilson felt uneasily that he would have a disturbing obligation to look efficient himself, now that he had so smart a chap at his elbow. He felt like someone being awakened and pulled out of bed.

He got up and put a pencil behind his ear with an air of one who was putting some essential bit of mechanism into place before he began to think. Then he strode desperately into the warehouse, for in spite of that adjustment the mechanism did not begin to work at once. Then like an inspiration he remembered that in theory the boxes were arranged in series of types and sizes. Although few boxes found their way to the proper spot, he had once drawn a little plan which showed where they should be. It was on this theoretical disposition of things, not on the reality, that he began to discourse.

Christopher Homm followed this eloquent minister between the rows of boxes, not listening to the disquisition but letting it fall over him like a spray. He did not grasp its meaning but he sensed its lack of accord with the muddles about him. As Mr Wilson strode on, growing more eloquent, Christopher Homm followed with a slowly developing grin of disbelief and triumph.

XIV

IN ENTERING UPON REGULAR EMPLOYMENT AT THE
warehouse Christopher Homm was giving up one conception
of himself. He had sustained several years of intermittent and
casual work because he had elected to think of himself as a
prophet. He denounced society not in the name of God –
whom he declined to know – but of several abstractions which
he drew as a veil between himself and the Divinity. These
qualities or mere names were like banners thrown across the
whole sky. Humanity, justice, freedom – the words spurted
hugely out of his mouth as he stood on his open-air platform
addressing whomever would listen.

Not many would. His thin long fingers could be seen
clutching the wooden lectern, and his body seemed to hang
below it to the small transportable platform, but the head
that nodded over the top showed too indeterminate a zeal
to hold the attention for very long. Christopher Homm
seemed less to be haranguing an audience than expressing
his own agony. There are few connoisseurs of this romantic
art.

"The condition of 'umanity" – and the people passing
seemed to him like sheep – "is disgusting. If they won't do
nothing but just carry on the way they are" – and he watched
them going about their business with scarcely a flicker of
attention for so queer a preacher – "what can they expect?"
His resentment mounted. "What can they expect? They are
trampled down" – and the quiet, well-fed grandmothers,
benign at least to themselves, looked up in surprise as they
carried their shopping baskets towards the quotidian battle –
"they will be trampled underfoot if they are not prepared

to . . ." It was at the point where his denunciation should have been followed by some indication of a remedy that Christopher Homm's discourses became most hesitant. His little group of co-operators had become so thin precisely because he had not been able to believe for very long in any of the remedies commonly preferred, and was himself neither ingenious nor deceitful enough to invent others of his own. "If they are not prepared, I say," he would go on wildly after a pause, "to snap themselves out of it, they will stay as they are and rot."

Christopher Homm's one regular attendant was a man with thin hair and a mackintosh who stood under the lectern facing in the same direction as the speaker, so that any passer who stopped for a moment to listen had to be bold enough to withstand not only the impassioned wobbling head of the speaker but the blank subnormal stare of the acolyte. Usually such passers were asking themselves whether the man on the platform was a politician or a man of religion, and usually they were impelled to move on before they had resolved this question. In the mind of Christopher Homm, however, there was no doubt about this matter. He was, he thought, a practical reformer.

"Humanity does not want words," ran one of his favourite perorations. "It doesn't want windbags, there's too many of them in the world already. What it wants is deeds, and when people realize that perhaps something will be done." But as to how, or by whom, or what, the speaker was silent or at any rate not specific. "Someone will have to make a start some time and the sooner it is the better it'll be for everybody."

Now and again someone who knew a little of Homm's history would appear at this point and begin to heckle.

"Oo tried to stop them as 'ad started?"

It was a question that would turn Homm's peroration into a fresh beginning. He assumed a frightened and aggressive benignity. The fingers clutching the lectern became white; the head wobbled over further into the auditorium.

"My friend," he would say, "if some of your mates 'ad done 'alf as much as I've done in the cause of 'umanity I'd be at their side now. But if any man says to me – an' some of them 'ave said it –" he added in the voice of one imparting a shameful confidence – "that there's not to be any such thing as freedom until they 'ave it their way, that man" – and in the mind of the speaker the singular stood for the half-circle surrounding him like a pack of wolves – "that man is a liar and I don't care who hears me say it."

"You want to stop that lick-spittle talk and come down off there! The workers of this country know what to do to a man who is a traitor to his class."

Occasionally Homm's declaration would draw some such fire from a fanatical unsmiling face, but more often there was no-one to care much what he said or to make out what so vague an orator had the power to betray or be loyal to.

When at last he got down from his platform Christopher Homm would look very tired. He and his acolyte would dismember the platform and lectern and carry the pieces off to their committee-room round the corner.

It was called the committee-room because that is an appellation of some dignity, but there was in fact no committee unless Christopher Homm, the acolyte, and the shoemaker in whose shop the platform was left constituted one. The shoemaker very rarely appeared in the street, and when he did it was in such disguise of a best suit and an overcoat that none of his customers would recognize him. The life he lived was, therefore, apart from the interchanges he had over the counter, a lonely one. He was a man of thought behind his steel spectacles, and because his isolation had led to timidity he liked to think of Christopher Homm as an emissary who might carry his thought into the great world. He knew that no reality answered very closely to this conception, and that the man who carried his platform out into the street could not comprehend, much less reproduce, the ideas that flickered in and out of his own head as he took the nails one by one from his mouth and banged them into whatever he had on his last. But the unreality of Christopher Homm's missions did not render them less objects of excitement and concern to the shoemaker. They remained a ceremonial re-enactment of the sending of the dove from the ark. Against all hope the shoemaker expected that one day some astonishing reality would be infused into their ceremonial character. The ark might even touch ground on Ararat.

The shoemaker would look up from among his litter of shoes when Christopher Homm came back. It was the moment of Christopher's greatest importance, though he felt that it was an importance in which he had only the hollowness of a symbol. Merely to stand for something important, without understanding exactly what, made Christopher Homm dream, and his special significance was emphasized by the bearing of the acolyte who, at such moments, paused deferentially in the doorway looking so empty that a gust could have blown him away.

"Did you get many to listen to you?" The shoemaker was genuinely anxious, as if about the fate of a message of his own.

"There was a few." The tone was meant to add: "more than you would have expected."

The shoemaker had the kettle boiling and while Christopher Homm and his companion put away the pieces of the lectern he made tea in a squat blue enamel teapot and put three cups on a corner of the counter. It was a sign that he was preparing for philosophical discussion.

In the face of such preparations Christopher Homm began to look at once more important and more uncertain. It flattered him to be addressed as he was about to be, but why was it that, faced with the tough and twisted little shoemaker, he became always nothing more than an audience?

"The mind," the shoemaker would begin, "is more like the body than anything. If I go out there in the street without my clothes" – and the shoemaker looked out through the dirty window pane as if he really contemplated this enormity – "a bobby'll soon enough come and have me locked up. But it's only nature. The same with the mind. If I go out there, dressed with a lot of lies, no-one'll take any notice. But let my mind go naked like . . ."

As the shoemaker went on, he adumbrated the existence of a social conspiracy directed against Homm and himself, the supposed vessels of inexpressible truth. The moment a man achieved anything, he ceased to be part of the persistent nonentity in which alone value resided. Anything achieved had been achieved at the expense of the basic protoplasm, anything expressed was expressed in a voice that, because it was of a person, could not be true to anything so impersonal. The shoemaker's glasses winked; it was as if he were a sparkle on an otherwise undifferentiated sea. His head and shoulders would appear from it, and gradually his whole streaming form would begin to rise. And then he would realize that by such thought and eloquence he too must become untrue, and it was with the softest of gestures that he would fall back into the grey, and Christopher Homm would find himself facing a man so still that he might have been merely leather.

The eloquence of Christopher Homm, out of a long political habit, always tended towards some action that would set the world to rights. Christopher did not particularly wish for eminence, but it is a quality of eloquence that it inflates the speaker. Listening to the quiet words of the shoemaker he felt himself to be in the presence of a reproof.

When Christopher Homm got down from his platform at the street corner there was a sudden break in time because his rattling words clashed with the ensuing silence. But to the words of the shoemaker silence seemed to be a conclusion in logic as well as in time.

Christopher Homm could hardly bear this conclusion, for although he expected to find his bliss in peace, this peace was too like an emptiness. Uneasily he would take his leave, receding from the philosopher as if he had been some impersonal enormity. The acolyte disappeared like an evanescence, and Christopher Homm made his way back to Torrington Street.

"Have you been out spouting again?" Felicia did not think much of this as a contribution to her liberation from the troubles that assailed her. A little wad of pound notes, she basely thought, would do more for the human spirit.

It was a relief for Christopher Homm to find himself once more in a personal battle. The empty spaces of the shoemaker's philosophy were filled at once by the large body of Felicia and her powerful spirit. It was as if she presented physical boundaries within which he could walk and struggle, and at the same time breathed into the whole world of his perceptions a quality which was ineluctably human. He knew that he could not produce his abstractions before her. He entered instead upon a contest of pride.

"You call it spouting," he would reply. "All you think about is what you're going to eat and what hat you'll wear."

"And I suppose you don't care about eating? You'd be the first to complain. It's a wonder you get anything, the money you bring home."

Felicia was unjust in her accusation, for Christopher Homm was so lost in his imbecilities as to care little enough what he ate.

"And as for hats," Felicia would go on, feeling herself here to be on surer ground and full of a justified bitterness, "When did I have a new hat? Not in years! It's all I can do to send Sue to school looking as if she belonged to anybody."

This was meant to hurt. Felicia knew that philosophy was nothing to Christopher Homm beside the fate of his small daughter, and all the time she was seeking to discover what it was which none the less kept him at his preaching while the girl went without. It was that Christopher was so far advanced in his philosophy that he did not wish to give any superfluity even to his daughter. At this epoch his life was of a puritanical strictness.

For hours Christopher and Felicia would talk on and grow bitter with each other. The resumption of this long quarrel comforted Christopher for it gave him once more specific objectives and rendered his world provisionally intelligible.

XV

BEFORE HE HAD ENCOUNTERED THE PLEASURES OF
self-expression or felt the chill of a philosophic encounter,
Christopher Homm had indulged in committees and con-
spiracies. The "committee room" he then frequented was
peopled by real participants in intrigue. They would sit
round the big kitchen table covered with a green cloth, their
hands on the table, concentrating like a party awaiting the
operations of a medium. The dark figures were individual-
ized only while they spoke, and when they had spoken they
relapsed as it were into the syrup of conspiracy.

The chairman was a man who had been handsome, but
whose skin had been drawn outwards and downwards as if
by a bulk of heavy liquid inside him, so that his face, and the
whole of his seated person, had the shape of pears. His
mouth was one that liked to utter oppressions. When he
introduced a topic, it was with an almost complete im-
mobility of countenance; liveliness he kept for the scorn he
must use when he heard what his fellow-conspirators said
about it.

His hands clasped before him, he moved his lips ever so
slightly and let out a few words. They ran to the middle of
the table and stopped, mice for five watching cats to play
with. For a moment all the watchers were still; that man had
need of courage who was to speak first after the chairman.
Then a bald-fronted man, with fuzzy wig-pieces above each
ear, became more clearly visible and lifted his large and heavy
head. The mask showed all the conscienceless determination
of vanity. It marked no settled conviction but personal
ambition. The speaker's hesitancy in beginning was merely

a doubt which way he would strike hardest. It was a sleight to hide that he would strike the chairman, for he could not sit at the same table as any superior. The chairman passed the tip of his tongue over his upper lip as a sign that he acknowledged the challenge and was unperturbed by it. That was the moment at which he came nearest to smiling.

The challenger took the chairman's words and tossed them gently into the air. There was nothing murderous or otherwise final about this movement. It was the first formal movement of a game, like a pawn to the king's fourth. After this preliminary action he stopped. It was early to bode victory but he meant his fellow-conspirators to understand that the matter was already concluded. The man on the chairman's right drew imperceptibly nearer to him, declaring his allegiance. That man's neighbour threw in the same direction a glance that, if it had not been instantaneous, would have been insolent. The challenger flicked an eyelid to notice it; he too had his man. The eyes of all four men turned suddenly to Christopher Homm. He held the balance by a vote.

Christopher Homm's loosely-joined bones rustled altogether in their sockets. The soiled fair skin drawn over them twitched, and lips and eyelids for a moment quivered while their owner was concocting a thought. He had the weakness of a man who can perform this feat only under the stimulus of an emotion. At that moment he was at the mercy of a most unpractical indignation.

When Homm's fellow-conspirators perceived that he was merely indignant they relaxed into a luxury of contempt. Whichever side he chose to speak for, what was said out of righteousness could not advance the matter. They saw that any discourse he made could only give them time to prepare a final battle among themselves. Christopher Homm, however, did not appreciate his own irrelevance. All the lengthwise bones in his body became longer and thinner. He was about to indulge in an act of heroism and he was afraid. His hands as he waved them in the air split into fingers up to the wrist. Beneath his translucent jacket one could see his ribs caging a palpitating heart.

This heart, rather than his thick, inconvenient tongue, was the seat of Christopher Homm's eloquence. His speech had fire but it had not number. Such certainty as he possessed did not belong to the matter in hand but to a world he could see as little as could his companions. On the issues under discussion Homm had nothing to offer but mistakes, tergiversations, vituperations. He was conscious of his nobility in this confusion. His hands waggled; his head nodded; his eyes looked bloodshot. As he spoke peace grew among his fellow-conspirators. They could unite at any rate in contemning him.

When the chairman resumed after Christopher Homm's outrage it was almost in good humour. That simple man's passion had disturbed the malice of the agenda. The evil could not be made perfect until he was evicted, and that would in itself be a pleasant operation.

The chairman did not speak to any of Christopher Homm's turgid arguments. Instead he started a measured denunciation in the tone of one beginning a black mass. His murmuring speech went from stage to stage in perfect order, and grew almost imperceptibly to a cold anger in which his words were suddenly at Christopher Homm's throat. The hero choked and waggled his hands hopelessly. The chairman shook away from him and another of the conspirators began to speak. He too used gentle words which in a moment became ferocious, and he too ended by shaking that weak and unsuitable body.

When he had finished there was a silence, and Christopher Homm had either to surrender or to grow more angry. It was neither courage nor calculation, but the mere pleasure of letting his blood boil over, that provoked him to make a stand. For an instant he was almost magnificent. He rose half out of his chair and raised one hand above his head. He reminded himself of a print he had seen of an incident in the French Revolution, and that self-consciousness destroyed his power. A mere boiling of the blood may be a conviction, but a dramatic action is politics. Once back in that world of manoeuvres, Homm re-established his inferiority immediately. He was then little more than a corpse to be removed from the arena.

He was, however, a corpse with some fight in him. When the conspirators turned on him to lump him physically out of the room he struck out till his fists bled first at one and then at another. It was not easy to pin his arms behind his back. His ejection was uncertain until someone pulled off the green tablecloth and put it over his head. He struggled a moment, and then he was quiet like a parrot whose cage has been covered.

When Christopher Homm found himself in the street he hardly knew whether he had undergone a defeat or a triumph. On the whole he inclined to the latter view. He had knocked several people about and that in itself was delightful. This exuberance gave him a conviction that people might still be made to listen to him. He made his way up to the first group of his mates he saw standing on a street corner and began to address them.

"Those buggers in there have been getting tough." He expected support. But the louche-eyed group looked at him suspiciously from under the peaks of their caps.

"What you been up to?" they asked. Christopher Homm felt that he was in a world of devils.

Another group was standing in the brimstone on the other side of the street. Christopher Homm moved over to them and began to stir them a little more cautiously.

"What d'you think they've been up to in there?"

The members of this group looked at Christopher Homm's thick lip and sweaty hair. They shuffled, and it was a small dark man who spoke destructively:

"They bin telling you where you get off by the look of it."

The other members of the group laughed, happy to be able to attend to a joke instead of to the bedraggled enthusiast before them. The weasel saw his advantage and followed it with a more malicious violence:

"They know a sneaking lick-spittle when they see one. Don't you come round here mate, you'll get some more."

The others in the group could not counter this violence. They stirred uneasily like consciences wrapped in sleep. Christopher Homm could not be received into this group because one man stood at the entrance with a fiery sword. He stood on one leg at the edge of the pavement, the foot of the other leg swinging over the gutter. For a moment he had the appearance of a thoughtful man. But he was vincible and when his loose foot regained the ground it was to begin to take him further down the street.

As he passed along he saw the open door of a cookshop. A little steam came out as if from an odoriferous washday. He went in and slipped into place on the bench before an almost empty table. The back of the bench was a partition that shielded him from most of the customers. He could see only the road and the one man sitting opposite him. By turning his head he could be aware that he was sitting under the battlements of a counter surmounted by glass cases of show-cards and sandwiches. He could guess that the steam came from some apparatus against the wall beyond.

"Do they have hot dinners here?" he asked the man opposite him, less because he wanted to know than because he wanted to metamorphose that man's stare into an exchange of conversation. The question was unexpectedly successful. The staring opponent became a quiet family man accustomed to care for others.

"The best thing to 'ave here, if you want something hot, is one of them meat puddings," he said. Christopher Homm was a bit slow to show any gratitude but he felt that he must do so, so after a while he replied:

"I don't want much, only a cup of tea and something."

His adviser was not so easily put off.

"You can't always eat the meat in them," he said, "but the gravy is good. I always have one for something hot."

At this moment a large, fatty face and bosom leaned over the counter and said:

"What jew want mister?"

The "mister" was a touch of hostility rather than of respect. It showed that Homm was not a regular customer.

"I only want a cup of tea," he said, feeling desperate as he had done before his neighbour at the table had comforted him.

"Is that all?" The woman was practically asserting that it was not enough, and she looked as if she would not withdraw until there was a further order.

"I'll have a meat pudding," said Christopher.

"Chips." The woman was announcing that he would have those too, and she disappeared.

"I don't have the chips." Christopher Homm's neighbour began an analysis of his economy. "I bring sandwiches like it's cheaper and then just have the meat pudding for something hot. I cut them when I go out in the morning 'cos the missis doesn't get up much like now. Then I can manage it on tenpence with the pudding."

Christopher Homm became aware of domestic problems being laid before him for inspection.

"There's plenty that don't get a living wage," he said, "and the buggers'll never give it till they're forced to."

This comment did not break at all upon the bursar's contemplation.

"If you reckon so much for dinners and so much for fags you know where you are like. Then the missis 'as got to 'ave some special stuff the doctor said and I've got to put so much aside for that." The man seemed proud of his feat.

Christopher Homm now had his meat pudding and chips and his cup of tea before him. His neighbour looked at the plate critically:

"They ought to 'ave given you more gravy. You want to ask for some more."

Christopher Homm put his knife and fork into the soggy pudding. At first it bent inward without breaking, and when he withdrew the implements it gradually resumed its original shape. The man who had recommended this delicacy watched its movements with interest. He was anxious to see whether it corresponded as it should with the account he had given of it.

Christopher Homm's knife and fork descended on it again. This time they passed the outer skin and brown blood began to ooze from it. Both spectators watched curiously. A further pressure produced a wide rent and a little puff of savoury steam came out. Christopher Homm opened his mouth in preparation for the treat and then hoisted a bleeding fragment on his fork and clapped it in. It had beside a taste of hot pepper and salt a rare flavour of garbage.

"'Ave some sauce if you want it." The woman had re-appeared and was handing Christopher a bottle. He shook a few blots of it on to his plate and went on eating. The man opposite him was now silent, as a member of the family might be because there was nothing either to explain or to complain of. Christopher Homm felt happy.

XVI

IF FELICIA DID NOT ADMIRE THE ELOQUENCE WHICH
Christopher had learned to expend upon politics, still less
had she admired the activities of earlier days when he had
been useful without being useful to her.

In the employment he then had he drew, besides his pay,
a little emolument of self-importance. He had the illusion
of being valued by his employer because of the way he did
his work and by his fellow-workers because he defended their
rights better than they could themselves. The former estimation Felicia could smile on, because there was always a
possibility that it might turn into banknotes or at any rate
into half-crowns. The latter seemed less a vanity in her
husband than a cruelty, directed of course against herself.
Christopher was making himself strong to fight in a battle in
which she was not concerned, and she felt thereby deluded.

Homm's employment at this time was in a wholesale
tailoring and dressmaking business. Two high workrooms
under yellow electric lamps constituted its manufactories.
In one, the heads of women and pale girls bent over sewing-
machines or needles and a sea of patterned materials. In the
other, thin bowed men with tape-measures and large scissors
gathered round tables on which were extended flat and inani-
mate bodies of blue serge. Christopher alone among the
employees had the right to circulate at will through these
domains and to penetrate into the garage that lay beyond.
He sometimes drove the van housed in this fastness, and he
excused himself from work for many an hour by pretending
to tinker with it. He packed up goods that were to be des-
patched and checked over the newly arrived bales of

material. He occasionally won the liberty of a stroll in the street carrying intimate messages from Mr Samstag.

Mr Samstag by a gesture could give the workrooms as he walked through them the air of an oriental bazaar. His great copper smile and enormous, flashing hands sailed through the mid-air as he passed. When he stopped to speak his body bent forward from the waist, for he was anxious and appeared flattered to hear the scarcely coherent responses that his staff made to him through embarrassed, hardly opened lips. In reply to the visiting attention of Mr Samstag, the work-people in both the rooms were like a peasantry who would scarcely look up from their quiet grazing. The more he flashed with wit or even kindness the more inarticulate they became. He could make them drift like sheep but he could hardly obtain a more specific response.

It was to this puzzled shepherd that Christopher Homm became a guide. When the body of Mr Samstag bent forward, and the smile and hands signed themselves like a great initial on the air, Christopher Homm would often pause uncertainly beside him. It seemed as if whatever was trans-mitted between Mr Samstag and his workpeople passed through the intermediary of that figure whose activity was in his waveringness.

"Do ze work quick," Mr Samstag might be urging, "oderwise we get no more bisnis." The plea would be lost in the upper and obscurer parts of the room unless Chris-topher, with a little smile, recaptured it. The workpeople felt that they must ignore so direct an instruction. Their eyes were downcast upon their work when they heard it and their hands practically ceased to move. An obscure honour im-pelled them to disobedience. Their shame became even greater when Mr Samstag, wishing to produce at once an explanation of his command and a proof of his generosity, said:

"I pay you. Certain I pay you if you work quick. We all get more bisnis."

As if that mattered, the reluctant contempt of the work-people seemed to say. It was indecent even to mention the possibility, and the proferred bribe was an attempt to bind them to this unimportance. At such moments they were near to putting down their needles and in fear retreating at once into stillness and liberty. It was Christopher Homm who, by a little gesture and a smile, suggested that it might be safe to accept the dubieties their employer uttered, that at any rate they should not be rejected until Christopher had thought whether they could be turned to advantage. It was in the women's workroom that Christopher Homm's action was most electric. He seemed to these inchoate creatures to be charged with a reassuring power. They would wait; they would be safe; he would if necessary protect them. Mr Samstag and Homm moved on, and the women resumed their grazing.

Sometimes the women, rather to test their safety than because of any real grievance, would make what they would pretend was an incurable trouble. Murmurs would start between two of them in one corner of the workroom, and they would be taken up by one and then by another. Sometimes the same complaint or rumour would slumber and dream among them for days at a time, and then wake so that the murmurs became louder and at last broke into shrillness. At such moments Mr Samstag would appear from his office with a face that no longer shone and with hands embracing one another not in glee but in anxiety. He would fear that he was losing both profit and affection, and he felt for both losses with equal desperation.

In this distress Mr Samstag could not address the women. He merely looked at them as if he were about to cry. He would then wring his hands and look about him until Christopher Homm appeared.

This was the moment of Christopher's Homm greatest significance. Mr Samstag would look to him as if for comfort and it was Homm's rôle to treat him to an enormous display of scorn. The women blew together like standing corn and said to one another that he was not afraid.

"What do zay want? What do zay zay?" In such moments Mr Samstag freely admitted that communication between himself and his employees was impossible.

It was rare on these occasions for Christopher Homm not to find himself briefed with a reply. If he was not, he would move among the women, stopping and bending here and there to listen, until he possessed enough of their grievance. Then he strode up to Mr Samstag and made his demand.

"They won't go on working in this material. It's too hard on the hands."

Or: "They can't have their tea in ten minutes and they're not going to try any more."

Whatever Mr Samstag produced to counter these demands Christopher Homm was merciless. He pretended to be so much a man that Mr Samstag softened into feminity before him.

"You can take it or leave it, Mr Samstag. They won't put up with it. It's either that or walk out."

Mr Samstag would retreat miserably into his office and Christopher Homm would turn to advise the women.

"Don't haggle with him." That was always the gist of what he said. Mr Samstag would turn the place into a market and outwit the women with some plausible offer.

At these times Mr Samstag liked to send Christopher Homm out with a message. He would hope to settle this little matter before the champion returned. But neither he nor the women had any confidence in the settlement they had made until Christopher Homm had blessed it. Mr Samstag would enquire of him with genuine anxiety.

"Are zay satisfied now? I can't do no more for zem."

It did not depend on the merits of the case, but on Christopher Homm's humours of the moment, whether he allowed matters to rest at the settlement or encouraged everyone to be awkward.

"There's got to be someone to stand up for them," he would explain to Felicia in the evening, "they're not organized."

The sense of the last remark was not plain to Felicia, who understood it as some general slight on women.

"So they can't manage without you," she said with a sneer. It seemed improbable that her husband could be of any use to all those women. He was not much use to his wife.

But Felicia was more concerned when Christopher reported that there was trouble with one of the girls. She was going to have a baby.

Felicia dropped her teacup into her saucer and said:

"You been messing about with her?" Her tone was only superficially anxious because she did not imagine that any of Christopher's real sins would be put to her so boldly.

Christopher was nobility itself.

"I'm merely *acting* for her," he said.

"A girl like that," said Felicia. "You let her act for herself. I bet she knows how all right."

Christopher had a juicy story to unfold. "The trouble is," he said, "it's old Samstag."

Felicia did not see that it made any difference who it was. She had always thought Samstag must be a bit of a dirty dog. There must be something wrong with him anyway if he thought half as much of Christopher as she was told he did.

"It's upsetting them all down there," Christopher explained. That was the reason for his intervention. It showed him in an amiable light. Felicia knew that her husband must have some base motive for his interest. It was difficult for her to believe that merely standing up for others gave him the illusion of being himself just. So her first superficial anxiety deepened.

The girl who was the subject and centre of these disturbances was not remarkable for her beauty. She was a slight sandy child with her limbs so skewered that she appeared always to be going sideways. Her eyes were pale and without love. She had not even tried to give a false amorousness to her lips. But for the plumping of her belly, which she did not dress to conceal, one would never have thought of her in a bed for two. She seemed drawn together by a resented ugliness.

Marcy was taciturn and the scandal grew around her silence. The women drew away from her and made up stories about her to satisfy their lust and malice. The colourless, suffering girl became ingenious and evil.

"You can see the sort she is. She's the sly, quiet sort. She'd always be finding someone to mess about with her."

They gazed at her with hatred and in their talk they undressed her.

"I don't see why they find her attractive. She must be a skinny, twisted little bit."

"Jew know who she said done it?"

"Whoever it was I bet he wasn't the only one."

"Jew know she said it was Mr Samstag?"

The woman who thought of that enjoyed a triumph that was almost too great for her. The others cooed and cackled with delight.

"She said that?"

"Jew know it's old Samstag? I wouldn't let 'im touch me."

"You'd think she'd have more self-respect."

The entrance of Mr Samstag sent the women back to their places, where they fixed their eyes on their work and their hearts on this disgraceful secret. Christopher Homm, who had been moving about the outskirts of the workroom and had heard enough to hope for a criminal excitement, looked at his employer with a new admiration. Fancy him doing that! Then he apprehended that it was only as a defender of decency that he could have any rôle to play here. So he changed his gaze to one of puritanical scorn.

Mr Samstag appealed to him dumbly to explain this excitement. The scorn of Christopher Homm became colder. It was evil and delightful to be so venomous. The venom poured into his heart from one tap while a righteous zeal poured in from another. Mr Samstag waited, vaguely aware that on this occasion he must expect more than a mere transmission of disgruntlement.

Christopher Homm was, in a sense, acting as the emissary of the conspiratorial women who bowed over their work and scarcely looked up. But the indignation they had collected among themselves was merely a medicine Christopher Homm took a spoonful of before he started to dance to the destruction of Mr Samstag. The humours that worked him into the final passion were his own.

Mr Samstag stood at the door of his office, looking pale, and Christopher Homm, within sight of him, moved round the edge of the workroom. When he had approached in one direction near enough for Mr Samstag to suppose that he was about to be addressed, he sidled back and, traversing perhaps the whole circumference of the room, approached his employer from the other side. He would have performed this figure of his charming and menacing dance a number of times if Mr Samstag had not had the presence of mind, the second time he was approached from the left hand, to call out:

"Hier a minute Homm. I wanntt you."

This was a challenge which Christopher Homm, in full view of the workroom, could not for his vanity ignore. He gave Mr Samstag a physical obedience, by approaching him, but then full of terror and drawing himself up to his full height, said:

"I want to speak to you, don't worry."

Mr Samstag partly apprehended the insolence of the idiom and said in a quick dignified voice:

"I not worry. It iss you who worry. Now what for you worry? Ant these ladies?"

"Look here Mr Samstag we better not talk here."

Mr Samstag was glad enough to withdraw to his little office where he could talk to Homm across a table. Homm had never sat down in the office before, but now he was invited to take a chair. That invitation was as good as a confession of guilt.

He sat back and looked at his employer with a puzzled self-importance. He imagined that he was powerful enough even to pity him. As Mr Samstag said nothing he at last began encouragingly:

"Well, Mr Samstag, what are you going to do for Marcy?"

Mr Samstag looked genuinely puzzled for a moment and then decided to resolve this disagreeable condition by growing angry:

"What do you mean? I do for Marcy? What iss zat to do wiz you? You are impertinent."

Christopher Homm, in a perfect dream of greatness, lolled over towards his employer with a great charitableness:

"Look here Mr Samstag you know you got to settle something pretty decent on her?"

"Settle? I settle? What you mean? I pay her her waches!"

Christopher Homm continued to be kind but grew more insolent.

"Look here old son you know you got to do something better than that."

Mr Samstag was still not seized of the point:

"But why I give a rice to her?"

Christopher Homm at that moment was fatter and more genial than he had ever been before. He saw himself, leaning on the corner of Mr Samstag's desk, as entering upon a great success. But this fatness and greatness was possible only because he was surrounded by no comprehension. It was as if he had expanded to fill a vacuum. The moment Mr Samstag understood what was being said to him Christopher Homm grew lean and shabby again. The bronze man stood up and shone. His picture of himself as a man living religiously for his family was being dishonoured.

"I gif you your money and you get out off here. You get out!"

Christopher Homm could not believe his ears.

"You get out! You get out!"

Mr Samstag gave him some notes that more than made up his pay. It was a sign that he was much moved.

Christopher Homm could find no words to defend himself with. He gave way, Mr Samstag pressing upon him and gesticulating, until he reached the outer door. It was nearly time for the workroom to be shut. There, on the other side of the road, was Felicia waiting to take her husband into custody. In a doorway a little way off a shapeless man hanging on crutches was watching for Marcy with burning eyes.

XVII

CHRISTOPHER HOMM DID NOT RELY SOLELY ON THE grievances and misfortunes of his workmates to give him importance. He also drew on his daughter Susan, whose childhood was overshadowed by his magnificence. His hollow, lolloping body, so empty of certainties, could be rendered solid and deliberate by the illusion that he was acting in defence of her.

There were days when Felicia's whole campaign was to harry her child. As soon as Susan awoke Felicia would say:

"Out of it, you lazy girl! Come on, quickly, or I'll smack your bottom."

The child would drowse and sulk on to the bedside mat, looking at her toes as if they were independent creatures. She was in a mood to wait for assaults.

"Come on, hurry!"

Susan's only response would be to push her other foot out from under her nightdress to examine it.

"Get something on, quickly!" Felicia would shout, standing over the child and waving her arms like a windmill toppling over.

The child, who now wished for nothing but that the wrath should visit her, curled up on the mat and went as if to sleep. Felicia prodded her with a ferocious toe.

"You lazy little devil get a move on or I'll tan you."

Through a multiplicity of screams and disorders the little family would finally arrive at a table laid for breakfast. In the half-darkness of the dining-room the savage faces of husband and wife would stare at one another over the chipped cups. Susan would loll on her chair in arrogant and sulky ease.

After an interval Felicia would begin to call out:

"Eat your breakfast and double quick. D'you want me to smack your bottom again?"

The child would take a leisurely mouthful and turn away. Just as Felicia's rage was mounting for a new assault Christopher, whose mind had hitherto swum in a lake of sleep and dejection, decided that he would insult his wife by pretending to be just. Knowing he had no merits of his own, he could yet grow resolute on behalf of Susan. He waggled his empty frame into a more rigid condition and spoke in a military voice to his wife.

"That's enough of that. You leave her alone."

Felicia hated to meet a resolution as pretentious as her own. For a moment she waited and hoped she had not heard aright. Christopher was encouraged by this. His body began to grow vigorous and he felt that his anger would do him more good than his breakfast.

"Someone's got to stand up for the kid." He stood up himself to indicate that he was the man.

To show her defiance Felicia reached out for Susan's arm. She intended to put the child across her knee then and there to illustrate her own notions of justice. At the same moment, however, Christopher seized Felicia's arm and upset a cup of tea over her dress as he did so. Felicia screamed as if the hounds were at her throat and tried to pull herself free. Susan darted behind her mother's back and got safely out of the room.

"You let go," Felicia shouted. "Laying hands on a woman like that. You ought to be ashamed."

"I'm not going to sit here and see my child knocked about for no reason at all." Christopher pretended to be utterly disinterested.

"Nothing at all!" screamed Felicia. "You seen the way she's been behaving. It's time someone took it out of her a bit."

Christopher relied on a chilly dogmatism:

"Unless the child's done something wrong don't you hit her."

The door banged outside. Susan, in horror at these occurrences, was running off early to school in the hope that it would be more like home.

Between husband and wife the tension was momentarily released. Christopher became aware of the pleasant firmness of the arm he was holding. Felicia's face, as he looked down on it, was flushed. It was more agreeable in this physical fury than when contracted to define the niceties of some command. A physical kindness might have supervened to displace Christopher's righteousness had he not had himself to go off to work. He was late already.

As he walked down the road his determination to stand up for the weak gave lightness to his step. He determined that that day it should go ill with Mr Samstag. Mr Samstag, however, turned out to be away, and the weak for whom Christopher Homm had resolved to do battle gossiped all day and were not interested in justice. He was so disgusted that he resolved to go in search of a wrong to be righted. He walked out in the mid-afternoon with no more definite intention than that, and he found himself passing Susan's school just as the children were coming out. He was touched to see his daughter, among so many laughing ones, looking sombre and oppressed. He went up to her.

"What's up, Sue?"

In the face of this misunderstood grief he felt diffident. In her turn Sue was rendered uneasy by her father's humility. As if guessing what would make a man of him, she complained of an injustice.

"The teacher said I ought to brush my hair and wash my neck. I don't think it's fair. The other girls all laughed and some of them was worse than me."

Christopher Homm looked at his daughter and for a moment hesitated in sympathy and embarrassment. Should he enter the childish world of this small trouble? It demanded the surrender of too much by a man who had set out to tilt at windmills. Christopher Homm hastily recovered the ebbing remnants of his anger. He would stick to the superficial world of outraged justice.

"Who was it said that to you?" His body recovered itself and his eye lit up as he found what he had all day sought. "Which teacher was it? Was it that fat one with glasses?"

Susan said it was and she then saw the folly of her confession. Her father was going into the school to tell the teacher off. Susan put screwed and anxious hands to her cheeks.

"You mustn't!" she said in agony. She hardly knew whether she feared that her father might not come back alive or that she would herself never dare to reappear on the scene where her father had interfered with Miss Mackerel's right to be unjust.

When Christopher Homm disappeared into the school Susan waited as if for an explosion. She pressed her slim back against the red-brick wall. It seemed to be the very end of life.

Christopher Homm moved steadily along the corridors of the school like the light on a fuse or a touch paper. He would find out this unjust woman and the explosion would take place. But the emptiness of the school began to affect his spirits. His boots were noisy on the concrete floor and the moment he began to walk on his toes he felt less bold. He peeped in the obscure cloakrooms and remembered in what agony one could be pressed against the hooks smothered in wet and sweating raincoats. He quickened his pace when he saw the daylight of the assembly hall in front of him. In his haste he bumped into a woman emerging from a door at the side of the corridor. At the first impact the woman pretended not to be there, for she was emerging from a lavatory. At a suitable distance from that disgraceful spot she turned and said to him in a prim voice:

"No one is allowed in here after school. Are you looking for anyone."

The tone was authoritative and softened by a mock concern. It suggested that Christopher Homm was an intruder both to the place and to the social class to which lady teachers belonged. Christopher Homm was not totally dismayed, but he had no anger and he had to direct himself to stay the course.

"I want to speak to Susan Homm's teacher," he said.

The woman dragged one foot back and received the reply with contempt. There were three hundred and fifty girls in the school and he should not expect his daughter to be known.

"Well it's her teacher I want." He chose to be unaccommodating.

The woman opened a door on the other side of the corridor. A burble of chatter and laughter came out: it was the staff room. She went inside and almost closed the door. Homm heard her say:

"There's a parent out here. He nearly knocked me over when I was coming out of the ladies'."

There was a burst of idiotic tee-hee-hees.

"Has anyone heard of Susan Homm? He says he wants her teacher."

"Is that that frightened looking little thing that never does her hair?"

"Yes, the skinny one. That'll be Miss Mackerel. She's gone, hasn't she?"

"Oh, well."

The door shut completely and Christopher Homm thought that was the end of it. He wondered whether they could get out any other way or whether he could wait and be rude to them when they emerged.

After a while the door opened and a short fat woman with glasses came out. Her figure was artificially contained and she looked like a stubby ninepin.

"Are you the parent?" she asked. "This isn't the time for them. Who did you want to see?"

It was established that he really wanted to see Miss Mackerel and that she was in the hall. The ninepin propelled him to the door and called out menacingly:

"Here's a parent for you, Miss Mackerel."

Miss Mackerel was pinning strips of paper on a blackboard at the other side of the hall. She turned on Christopher Homm with her lips studded with the brassy heads of drawing pins. She spoke such words of discouragement as she could without dropping the pins. Christopher Homm took no more than a step inside the hall.

The two looked at each other like boxers from opposite corners of the ring. Christopher Homm would probably be quicker on his feet but Miss Mackerel had more weight. It was of the kind that filled out the belly and the haunches rather than the bosom.

Instead of coming to blows at once the couple upbraided one another from their corners.

"It isn't the time for parents now," bawled Miss Mackerel and stood on her toes as if she were trying to get a better view of some child in a crowd at the other end of the hall.

"I'm a working man," said Christopher Homm, and the classification put a bit of fight back into a voice that had become dangerously submissive. "I can't come up here any old time."

Miss Mackerel resented both the fact that her opponent was a man, which she was not, and the fact that he should presume to claim that there was a merit in being of the kind known as working. Her eyes became very round and showed a lot of white about the pupil.

"Plenty of work goes on here. Don't you worry." She turned her back and resumed the pinning up of bits of paper.

It was an excellent defence. It was as if a tortoise had presented only the back of his shell to the enemy. Christopher Homm glared but felt that he could do nothing. He was no longer inspired by the spirit of justice. He was no longer there "on behalf of" his daughter. His problem was the more elementary one of getting out alive. He tried like Miss Mackerel to make use of whatever protection nature afforded. He assumed the air of a careless man not seeking to do battle. He leaned his back against the stage that was at the end of the hall, splayed his straight legs forwards and looked at his boots. In this casual attitude he might wait unnoticed until the enemy had gone and the school was empty.

Miss Mackerel, however, had not given up the battle. She was only waiting until her enemy became weaker. She turned on him so suddenly that, scuffing his feet together in an attempt to stand upright, he swayed and almost over-balanced. It was while he was still swaying that she began to move cruelly down the hall towards him.

"Well, what was it you wanted?" She rightly guessed that his desire could now be put in the past tense.

Christopher Homm had all he could do to stop himself from crying out "Nothing, nothing, it was nothing." Instead he put forward a tentative: "I was wondering if you was my little girl's teacher."

Miss Mackerel stopped and laughed as if the blood were dripping from her jaws.

"I teach a lot of little girls."

"I'm Susan Homm's dad," Christopher managed to say, and he could see at once that it was not a very important statement.

"Well," said Miss Mackerel. "Which one is that? What's she like?"

Christopher Homm thought of the child pressed in terror against the wall outside.

"She's rather a little girl . . ." he began.

"None of them are very big in my class. Oh, I remember, she's the one that never does her hair. She wants to wash her neck too."

Miss Mackerel took several paces forward and grinned at Christopher Homm. She tried to think of other opprobrious things to say about this man's daughter.

"It shows up the home the way the children are turned out."

This was better still. It was opprobrium for the girl and her father at the same time.

Christopher Homm showed a last bit of fight.

"She comes from a good home," he said. "We look after her."

Miss Mackerel chuckled as if all were well within her fat body but not elsewhere. Then she walked away smartly through a door at the further end of the hall.

Christopher Homm, bruised and frightened, crept out the way he had come. When he saw the light of the playground he let his boots clatter and he galloped.

Susan was walking slowly down the road. Homm saw, as she went, that there was nothing he could do to help her.

XVIII

ALTHOUGH CHRISTOPHER HOMM WAS SO EASILY
defeated it is not to be supposed that his life had been without
its military splendour. When he scratched around the backyard at Torrington Street on Sunday morning he still wore a
pair of old khaki trousers. He would put them on with a
certain sad pride, like a Chelsea pensioner arranging his
medals. Felicia, who suspected what illusions they represented
for him, used a tone of special savagery when she referred to
them dirty old army things.

She was that hostile spirit of truth which every man who
loves himself must seek to overcome. There was little
magnificence about Christopher Homm's arrayed figure.
The high-waisted khaki trousers, held up by his old coloured
braces, seemed even in their condition too comprehensive for
his skinny figure. Moreover it was evident that he put them
on not to work but to dream.

The dream had become a tenuous one that never now came
to any clarity of word or image. It expressed itself merely in
an occasional military rigidity of muscles of leg or shoulder.
That was all that was left.

But when Christopher Homm had first come out of the
army his life had been more vividly ambiguous. Dressed in
his ordinary clothes, he could walk down the road with what
appeared to him, though to no spectator, to be a military
pace. He would sometimes turn at a corner with a movement
which even a spectator would recognize.

At that time these barely overt movements of the body
supported a richer internal illusion. Christopher Homm
believed that he had been more useful than the people he

saw about him. He was amazed at and could resent the pul-
ullating streets that ignored that disciplined order of which
he had been a part. The tarts he was glad to see after living
in so masculine a society turned the way the money was as a
flower turns to the light. Boys too young to have been in the
war lounged with a step no sergeant had ever drilled, and
crept into corners with girls. Worst of all, men who had
flourished in factories and always slept between sheets while
he had been away presumed to have had grievances of their
own.

It seemed to him that, if not his usefulness, then the
deprivations he had undergone ought to be recognized in
some public manner. For a little while after disembarking he
felt that they might be, but it was less any civilian action that
pardoned this illusion than the infection of a general hope
among the soldiery. As he had marched through the streets
of the port it did not seem that the people who watched from
the pavements regarded him merely as a slave returning
from a deserved captivity. Once on a bus a conductress
refused his fare as if she were empowered to make a demonstration of generosity on behalf of the people. But such
distinctions were soon lost in the equalities of a large city.

Christopher Homm resumed his place in the competition
of appetites. As long as he was in uniform that was deferred.
It was then as if he had a religion which admitted him to a
fleshly communion. If he stood in a doorway sheltering from
the rain the dripping man in khaki beside him was nearer
than a brother. He could be held by a certain limited conversation rich in responses. It didn't seem to matter even if
the chap were an educated man with spectacles. Such a one
would drop his voice to the quiet undifferentiated tones that
all used.

"Where you got to get back to?"

"When you due in?"

A more complex exchange would start with the recognition of a regimental badge.

"How long you been with that shower?"

"Was you overseas with them? Where did you get to?"

Sometimes a patient neighbour would to pass the time begin one of those gentle collective boasts:

"I was with Z corps. Coo they was a shower. The syphilis boys they used to call 'em.

"The night they was supposed to embark they nearly broke up that bleeding transit camp. The officers had their revolvers out before it was finished. One bloke threw a beer bottle and hit a silly sod of an officer over the eye with it but though they threatened the whole ruddy lot of us they never found out who it was.

"D'you know one of those ruddy officers brought a tart into the mess and she was dancing there with nothing on. He was a lad, he was.

"If that had been you or me we'd have been in the ruddy guard room.

"Your feet wouldn't have touched the ground."

In these conversations the speaker had so little identity that Homm could imagine he was speaking the words of the better man who was his neighbour. He was, however, merely his own hope.

At no moment was that communion closer and the identification with his own hope more complete, than when he found himself marching in column. On a long march, like his companions he would set out with a grumble, but the talk would fall to nothing as the miles went by and the mind was put out. Then his leg swinging forward, carried on by the heavy boot at its extremity, gained momentum with the weight of fifty legs swinging before it. The slung rifle was nothing to retard him but something that added to his own bulk and power. Even the pack that held his shoulders back seemed heavy with a dynamo that drove him on. As the column swung round, so that the quiet men ahead of him appeared sideways on, what he saw was a grandiose and multiplied mirror of the hero he imagined he had become.

Long after these ranks were broken, and the men had gone discontentedly home to lose themselves in the superficialities of mere personality, Christopher Homm felt within himself the weight and force of this army. Had he encountered solid resistances, he might even by this grace have been able to overcome them. But he found merely an onrush of appetites of which he was invited to be one.

He was not so easily to be cheated of his glory. He would let himself quietly out of No. 92 Torrington St. and make his way to the main road. The trams that rode past him there were leviathans. The people swept on and would have swept him with them. But Christopher Homm saw that even when they followed a common direction they were a picture of discordances. They were united in nothing but in the following of their several appetites. This was not the society which he, with the sense of a military order within him, began obscurely to dream.

It was thus that Christopher Homm became a thinking man. The delusions of a mind slow to forget, but incapable of remarking clearly, he called his ideals.

It was on Felicia, preoccupied with her child, that he first essayed them.

"There ought to be more getting together." He would burble this after standing for five or more minutes in an attitude resembling thought. Felicia took no notice of thought.

"I mean," Christopher would go on, the agony of expression turning down the corners of his mouth and nearly bursting his heart, "not everyone going his own way but more mucking in like."

141

"You can muck in with me with that washing up," said Felicia. "That'll be a start."

Christopher did not like to see the generalities of a philosopher put to such base uses. In his stronger moments his two feet would take root where he stood and he would grow a wonderful foliage of thoughts. In his weaker moments, which came more frequently, he would give ground and seize a cloth to dry the tea things.

"I'm thinking of the larger unit." It was a grand sentence, and to illustrate it he would wave in the air the cloth still half-concealing a plate like a conjurer's property. The family domestic life, these were trivialities. Christopher Homm would build on a less manageable scale.

"For instance. . . ." He would enumerate those things which at the moment he most wanted. "The larger unit" he would say "Would give you all that."

There were times when Felicia felt that a larger unit was just what she wanted. "If it doesn't hurry up and give us whatever it is" she would say "we shall have to sell the few sticks we have got."

The particularist turn of Felicia's mind made her incapable of grasping general principles except as rods to beat her husband with. For Christopher these applications spoilt the whole pleasure of philosophy. He conceived of a philosopher as being above all a lazy man. So he would go and wander in the High Street.

It was evident from the little meetings that did take place on the various street corners that other exponents of the larger unit had also been turned out of doors by their wives. They gathered around speakers who had at least the gestures of passion and mingled reminiscences of the vanished communion of soldiers with promises of an impossible era. The unit described by the speakers became so large that in contemplating it the speakers resumed a comforting unimportance. They were not only anonymous but gagged and bound. It was delightful. The Larger Unit itself began to move. It had taken on a life of its own and the listeners clapped and cheered to think that they need no longer have any of their own.

It was after one such ecstasy that Christopher Homm resolved to play an active part. He told Felicia of his intention.

"I'm going to play a more active part," he said. "It isn't fair always to leave it to the other chap. After all we all benefit."

"Do we?" said Felicia. She did not know what form her husband's activity would take. It was so unlike him to display any activity in anything that she was not without curiosity to see what he would do.

Nor was Christopher himself. Then one day, as he walked down the High Street, he saw a little band collecting behind a banner. At first he thought it was the Salvation Army, and then he saw that they had neither uniforms nor hymn-books.

"March to Trafalgar Square." That was the invitation. It seemed a long way. Christopher Homm was about to pass when an angel stopped him. The angel had neglected to shave and had taken off his collar and tie, which still hung out of his pocket, in order to look more proletarian. He put his hand on Christopher's arm.

"This is your chance to play a more active part."

Christopher could see that at once. Yet he hardly had the impression that this was activity, when he fell in. The man who had pulled him into the crowd was active, certainly, with a quick dishonest smile and arms that seemed to be urging what, if they had been still, he could not have cared about. The rest of the party was idle and disconsolate. Only their words asserted that they were there of their own volition. The organizer had waved his arms and his followers came like rabbits out of a conjuror's hat.

"Do you think that it'll do any good?" Christopher Homm asked his neighbour in the ranks.

It was as if a man receiving the most expensive medical treatment had dared to question the value of it.

"'Ere, 'oo are you?" the neighbour replied. "What you in this for?"

There was a third man who understood perfectly the difficulties of beginners and was without any trace of honest indignation. His face was genial and false, like that of an unscrupulous nurse congratulating herself on having deceived a patient.

"It isn't the good that it does right away," he said, "and they will use every kind of blood-sodden treachery to stay where they are. We have to go on fighting and demonstrating until they can't hold out any more. This is just one battle."

He smiled and turned away, for what he had said was final. Moreover, he would rather repeat it to someone else than hear the formulation of the agonized doubts he could see crawling over Christopher Homm's face.

When the party moved off it was with the shuffle of men in loose bedroom slippers. Christopher Homm felt that he was not marching but going for a lonely walk, guards around him. The proximity and uncertain pace of the man in front made it difficult for him to keep his eyes on anything except a pair of heels.

"What about a song to put a bit of life into it?" someone asked.

The organizer did not reply to this address from the ranks, but the movements on the surface of his face indicated that it was not precisely life that he wanted. After an interval long enough for it to be supposed that the organizer had developed a volition of his own he began to lead off with:

> "*In the bloody maw of capital*
> *The boss will thrust you one and all;*
> *The babe is torn . . .*"

The picture Christopher Homm saw was of an agreeable carnage.

XIX

IT WAS A DIFFERENTLY REGULATED COLUMN WHICH, several years before, had taken Christopher Homm to the quayside where, in a dawn of unusual greyness, he had embarked upon his military adventures. The quiet waiting men had the air of slaves; it was the matelots, busy about the preparations for the voyage, who alone seemed to have life. The officers and N.C.O.s of the departing drafts appeared in a state between life and death, the spirit gone and with nothing to move them but a clinging sensation of duty.

Yet in the body of the slaves a sense of apprehension quickened, even though at that moment it could give no outward sign. The men eyed the gangway, guarded by military police, that would take them into the side of the great ship. At last a procession of orders began to pass along the waiting drafts. A party at a time, the men picked up their kitbags and their rifles and moved towards the gangway. Each party halted a little when it came to the brink of commitment, and as the men went into the ship the files appeared to be wasting like a dying virgin.

When Christopher Homm's draft came to the foot of the gangway he saw a murky hell within the ship. There were lights too dim to delineate, and blue men moving fuzzily within. The draft was the last to go aboard; his predecessors in the file might have been felled to a man when they disappeared. But when the encumbered Homm put his foot on the covered deck he found that he was in a queue, like any other, shuffling forward sulkily to an unknown destination. In time he had to climb a companionway. At the top the queue was still shuffling forward, this time between a deck-

146

house and the rail. There was water and cigarette ends in the scuppers. Soon a descent began. The men behind him seemed eager to come on but those below him slow, slow to descend. He arrived in a lighted and unbelievable world of closely packed tables and benches, over which disorderly troops were pulling their kitbags like ants with their eggs. But he had still to go down.

This time it was his own halting-place. He found himself assigned a place at a narrow table, with a man squeezed on each side of him and with rifles and kitbags everywhere. He supposed he was to mess here. Then he and his companions were instructed to stow their kit as best they could above their heads. They waited without instructions and then filed off in another queue to hand in their arms at the ship's armoury. By the time they had returned Christopher Homm had understood without being told that these few feet of mess-deck were all he was to live in during the voyage before him. A thousand men lay on the upper decks between him and the sky. Only the slender bulk-heads held out the airless sea.

The ship dawdled around the coast from port to port, as if Homm were aboard merely to be kept from land. Then in the mists of one morning he climbed to the open deck to see that he was in the midst of a convoy. It was almost joyous. A whole navy was moving with determination into the open sea.

The water was grey as metal but reluctant and unstable. A moist air came across the bows and the ship began to roll and be alive. For a few moments there was still a coast to fade. Then Christopher Homm was only a tick on a sea monster plunging into the deep.

Day after day they fared forward, crawling around decks awash with sea water and vomit. The world itself was sick as the massive Atlantic smashed against the sides of the ship

147

and she rose and fell with the precipitous waves. Now and then there was a crackle of guns, and the neighbouring ships rose to great summits or fell away out of sight as the terrifying contours of the sea demanded. Each day the men paraded dumbly on the decks beside the rafts that were supposed to save them if this shell should finally break apart and throw them upon the waters. Christopher Homm imagined himself clinging to one of these floats for the few minutes till the icy water made his body breathless and he was extinguished.

There were, moving about the upper decks, figures that had humanity and function, and the gunners in their turrets laughed and had teeth in their brown faces. But Christopher Homm was physical only to be sick; otherwise he was no more than a bare articulation among a herd of indistinguishable ghosts. No memories comforted him. It was only by hope towards an impossible future that he was Homm.

One day something exploded in that blindness and Christopher Homm was left scrabbling in the air with limbs of such hugeness that his toes reached the furthermost outriding destroyer. There was a low haze over the sea, which he saw below him mottled like a map of the moon. Through the moist air spars and bodies were falling, and as he himself drew nearer to the water he could see shoals of hungry round-eyed fish hovering below the surface; and under them a green world of caves and sea-growths. Imperceptibly his own bulk diminished, and it was as a small life-sized thing that he tore into the silky surface of a wave. Down he went through cold and bubbly water till he reached a stationary point of great pressure. It seemed to him here that he must crack like a bulkhead and the coldness irrigate all his ways, but without hope or apprehension he rose to an ordinary air lively with cursing and muscular men swimming arm over arm for the bobbing rafts. Here and there a stiller body sank resignedly from view.

Christopher Homm seemed to have an infinity of time to consider his actions; then he too struck out weakly and grotesquely towards a raft. As his movements grew slower it seemed to him that he was enacting strokes of enormous strength and that he would always have strength to continue. Suddenly everything on one side of him grew dark and as he turned he saw that he was on the flank of an enormous whale. Its dry leather grazed him as the creature turned. He was opposite inviting jaws and he struck out towards them as if towards safety.

When he was inside he found the whole mouth lined with some shining hard red substance, like the mouths of stuffed animals in a museum. He was scrambling along what seemed to be a huge curved tongue that disappeared into the gloom of a gullet. Above him hung the cavernous palate, fringed by stalactite teeth that were harmless because he was so far inside that they could not touch him. The tongue had some coercive power of its own and by its undulations it tumbled him forward toward the gullet. He had to be thrust into this darkness and he went with resignation. He was in an element thicker than air and very soft. Here no walls were needed to contain him; he was in suspense. Then he moved slowly downwards and onwards.

It was an agricultural whale and presently he found himself descending as if from encircling mountains into a land of green fields. Here he was to live and plough. Slightly behind him to his left, so that he had not at first noticed it, patiented a horse behind a plough that had already, as if by way of example, cut two initial furrows and part of a third. Christopher Homm went first to put his arm round the nose of the horse. He looked down into the thoughtful blue-brown eye and flicked away the strands of black mane that had fallen over it. The turned-down mouth was full of doubt and pity, and the animal had curled grey moustachios like those of some old labourer. He blinked and moved his jaws and shifted the bit. Christopher Homm gave him a pat and muttered to him, then turned back along the adjacent furrow and set his hand to the plough.

There was more than a day's work in that field. Each time he came up to one of the two hedges he was working between he drew a long breath that was partly satisfaction at the straightness of what he had ploughed and partly admiration for the work still to do. Each time he turned there was a musical shaking of the whole harness as if to mark up his score.

As he worked the sky turned from a clear blue, with small bright clouds traversing it, to a swept colourlessness banked towards the west.

"Come on," he said coaxingly to the horse. "One more and we'll turn in."

The horse went forward again with a slow nodding gait, and when he had done Christopher Homm left the plough in the furrow and walked away with so light a hand on the bridle that he was scarcely leading. Christopher Homm lifted the pole that closed the opening at the side of the field, and his feet and the horses' struck metal on the road. It was a narrow lane between hedges. Occasionally they found a rabbit ahead of them pausing in the middle of it. High overhead starlings circled as if wearily. An occasional bat flew within the walls of the lane.

Christopher Homm took off the horse's harness and bridle and turned him into a meadow. He closed the gate on an animal uncertain whether to eat or to stand resting, and made his way a little further down the lane. He hung the gear up in an open shed and went through another gate into a rough garden. In the window of the cottage an oil lamp was already burning. He passed the front door which was never opened and made his way round to the kitchen.

A woman of about sixty was working at the scrubbed wooden table. She looked up.

"You done a good long day up there," she said.

His own speech was slow and reluctant like his heavy body.

"Middling," he said.

"Is it finished?" the woman asked.

Christopher Homm lowered himself into the wooden armchair.

"It'll be pretty nearly another morning," he said.

The woman thought for a moment, and then said as if reproving herself:

"Oh, ah, it would be."

Christopher Homm did off his boots.

"You going to bed already?" the woman asked.

It was a sort of joke mingled with reproach and surprise.

"'Ave a bit of supper anyway."

The woman put a slice of cheese and a loaf on the table.

"'Ere, ain't you cutting it?" he said.

"You're impatient aren't you?" The woman's voice rang with humour and tolerance. She added a few more things to the table and Christopher Homm drew up his chair. There were thick slices of bread beside his plate, and he cut into the cheese.

"There's a bit of that pie cold if you'd like it."

Christopher Homm did not have to answer: he did not even have to lift his head. The remains of the pie were before him and he ate it out of the dish.

When he had finished he sat back and looked at the mantelshelf above the cold fireplace. Although the lamp showed the things only dimly he could distinguish every detail of the array. At one end was a white china vase with spills in it. It had a hard glaze partly overlaid with dust and was decorated with a spray of curly roses. Then came a cracked Toby

Jug with a black shining hat. There was a little clock next that did not go any more. Then a fawning china spaniel and a little girl in a poke bonnet falling over backwards to show her frilly drawers.

The lamp began to smoke and quietly and without panic the woman turned it down.

"Well, goodnight, mother." Christopher Homm got up and stretched before he turned to plod through the shady sitting-room and upstairs to bed. He needed no candle, for the moon shone into his room over the tree tops. There was a high iron bedstead, and a chest of drawers, and in a corner the luminous shape of a great water jug and basin. Christopher Homm stripped to his shirt and climbed into bed. The sheets were cool. On the opposite wall he could see the outlines of a text.

He turned to the window and dreamed towards the gauzes that were pulled across the moon. His eyes closed into a sleep as peaceful as his waking.

The light that woke him was yellower than the gold of the sun, and the west-country voice he heard was that of a short, dark, R.A.M.C. orderly standing beside his bed. He became aware of the throb of the engine. He was deep down in the ship, and far away aloft a bugle was sounding reveillé.

XX

IT WAS FROM A TOWN WHERE THE SOIL WAS LESS
bitter than in Torrington Street that Christopher Homm
had been drafted into the army. The house he and Felicia
there occupied gave directly on to the street almost opposite
the end of a bridge spanning a sizeable river. The surface
of the river showed traces of oil, and refuse gathered at its
walled banks. On the other side were great brick ware-
houses and an occasional crane. Trams creaked past the
Homm's door and over the bridge, but up the hill to the left
of it came, among the more raucous traffic, carts pulled by
quiet horses that still smelt of the villages they had set out
from. They would be driven by wary men bringing vegetables to the market, and they soon turned off into a side way
that took them into the place behind the Homm's house.
The market was about level with their chimney pots, and
this gave their tiny back yard the air of a prison exercise-
ground. Occasionally over the wall at the top would come
flying the discarded leaves of a cabbage or a piece of wet
newspaper.

"They're still chucking that stuff down here," said
Felicia. "Why don't you do something about it?"

Christopher once had. Badgered and reluctant, he had
climbed the steps on the other side of the house that led
straight to the market. A scaring fat woman with a coloured
handkerchief about her head stood at a stall by the wall
sorting cabbages and throwing the outer leaves hither and
thither. Her dress could hardly hold her skin nor her skin her
flesh. It was only by the concentration of her small mind in
her fingers that she managed to keep them moving, and if

that movement had failed her whole person would have become liquescent. Christopher Homm saw this and as he feared he pitied her. But Felicia had sent him, and he approached the woman with his open white hands hanging lax at his sides. The woman's mind remained in her fingers.

Christopher Homm had to throw back his head to carol his request to her.

"That's my backyard wall you're chucking them cabbage leaves over!"

Christopher Homm could be fierce enough to be ridiculous but not to intimidate. The fat woman rolled white eyes till their pupils were set on him. For a second her mind was on him and he felt it crawling over his head like a centipede. Then the woman saw that he was not a customer and tore another leaf off the cabbage she was holding. She looked at Homm to ask if that was what he meant and then threw the leaf over his backyard wall. Christopher Homm felt more enraged and more impotent.

"One time one fell on our baby's face in her pram!" he shouted.

"Her ma ought to know better than to put her down there," the woman replied, but she did not at once throw another leaf over the wall. She was protecting herself rather than attacking Christopher Homm or his baby. Christopher felt that he could be satisfied with that.

"Great fat woman," he explained to Felicia when he got back to the house. "I told her off."

It gave him satisfaction to be able to report that the criminal was a woman. It seemed to account for the fact that he had had to undertake this disagreeable journey. Felicia looked as if she scarcely believed that part of the story. It sounded to her more like a man's doing.

Christopher Homm and Felicia were just beginning to develop that hostility which they brought to such beautiful completion in later life. Felicia was not yet massive, and with her long thighs and sandy hair she seemed to match Christopher's own physique. They were a tolerable pair, no more; they could have stood naked together, in a marketplace for slaves, and just have avoided disgrace for their appearance if they had had their now toddling child between them as an excuse for being just past their first freshness.

There was a low gate across the open front door and it was over this that the snivelling Susan looked out into the great world. She looked out because of the interest of the legs passing on the pavement and because at this point she could feel safely that she had not wandered yet at the same time be at the very extremity of her world, in which trouble was sure to be brewing. If Felicia was not about to descend upon her perhaps both parents were thinking out one of those little experiments in hatred which they from time to time attempted. They made such experiments at this time with the diffidence of a yet younger couple making their first advances in love.

Christopher would see the young woman he had married preoccupied with some duty that gave her an excuse for not noticing him. The faintest of desires would come upon him to seize and come to grips with her person, as if to call back by force her vanishing girlhood. Then, knowing that an inopportune love would not be welcome he would give himself instead the pleasure of making her uneasy.

"You haven't wiped Sue's nose again she was all snotty when I come in." Felicia did not mind what mess her daughter's nose was in but she had a particular horror of the child being seen in that condition.

"Can't you see I'm busy trying to get you a bit of dinner?"

She would say this in justification of her neglect, but she had no intention of allowing any word of her husband's direct her to an action. She must therefore pretend to attach more importance to the duty she was in the act of performing than to the one she had failed to do.

When Christopher Homm sat down to dinner Felicia would feel free to go off to wipe Susan's nose. At this point it gave her a certain importance because it made her too busy to take her place opposite her husband at table. He would sit eating and reading his newspaper until the moment when Felicia stood poised over the child with a handkerchief. Then without seeing he would know that the moment had come to call out:

"Don't forget Sue's still out there with snot all over her face."

That would be torture to Felicia because she would not know whether to succumb in an act of obedience or to endure the disgrace of a dirty child advertising her incompetence. She would make up her mind by looking out into the street. If anyone who knew her was within sight she would savagely decide to wring the child's nose, and then go back and clear away her husband's first course before he had time to ask any question. But when she came back with his pudding he would ask, without even taking his head out of the paper:

"I suppose you've done it now?"

Felicia would be so angry that she could not enjoy her dinner, and that would be revenge enough for Christopher Homm for the supposed rejection of his incipient suit of love. But if there were no-one in the street that Felicia knew she would come back with an advantage. Then she liked to persuade the child to sit on its pot near the doorway so that she could bring back the used receptacle and the sight and smell of it mingled with Christopher's dinner. Christopher would protest, but in the weaker tone of one who had lost a battle.

"I don't know why I've always got to have that stink with my dinner!"

Felicia would bring it a little nearer his nose and shout triumphantly:

"You know I can't keep her waiting or I wouldn't catch it at all."

Christopher Homm would feel slightly sick and when he staggered back to work it would be Felicia who was left with the satisfaction of having accomplished her hatred.

Yet in the evening there would still sometimes be almost a concurrence of loves. The baby in bed, Christopher and Felicia would stand looking out of the doorway across the bridge on which lights were just beginning to twinkle. It was then that they both felt that they would like to go out for a walk, but they could not. Other lovers who had not yet undergone the consequences of their passion strolled past with arms round one another's waists. Christopher's love, which had not been comprehensive enough to cover both his wife and daughter amidst the squalor of their incessant needs, resumed the shape of almost adolescent longing.

But it was necessary to move from the station at the door. Felicia would be the first to go, pretending the claim of some duty that would give her the right to abstract herself from too close a union. Christopher would take a cigarette and add its rhythmic glow to the remoter lights before him. Sometimes a barge would pass down the river and Christopher Homm's longing would become unbearable. It was then that even he resolved to work.

For an hour or two husband and wife would be about the house at their several labours. At this time Christopher Homm still consented to polish the pram. It was a large, vain affair with metal and paintwork that could be made to shine, and he would work at it in the backyard with the light from the open kitchen door falling upon it while he crawled around it on the edge of the gloom. Felicia would be doing her ironing inside, heating the irons on the kitchen range that filled one wall. As she worked her face had the look of a thoughtful person's, but she was merely withdrawn. With her body employed, she could retreat and be nothing She was doing what had to be done; and even her husband was at the moment serviceable. Under the gas-light everything was safe.

Then a long-drawn cry would come from upstairs. Felicia would leave her calm and enter upon a fanaticism. She began by banging the iron heavily on the kitchen table and saying excessive things about the child.

"That child never has a wink of sleep all night long!

"Why can't Sue stay asleep when she gets there like any other child?"

It was a call for pity which Christopher Homm was quick to deny. He would come in from the backyard with a grim look and dirty hands threatening the clean clothes.

"Don't put your dirty hands on those clothes!"

From the fire which Felicia had lit around the baby she had now taken a torch to her husband.

"You leave her alone she'll be all right!" Christopher knew that this was the most offensive thing he could say because it implied that there was nothing that Felicia could do to quieten her daughter.

"Yes and have her yelling like that all night I suppose."

At this moment Felicia would imagine that she heard the bump of a baby falling out of bed. Without even a threatening look at her husband she would rush upstairs, leaving the doors open in the hope that they would bang.

Christopher Homm would wash his hands solemnly at the kitchen sink. It was not that he was preparing to help but he was getting ready to help no more. He wheeled the pram into the kitchen and put it in the most inconvenient spot between the kitchen table and the range where the irons were heating. Then he composed his face to a clever irony and moved to the foot of the stairs.

Here he waited in the shadows for Felicia to descend. If she came quickly, having quietened the child, he felt beaten. But if she was a long time upstairs, and then came down with Sue in her arms, he was triumphant. He would advance out of the shadows.

"Don't make me jump like that with the child, I might have dropped her."

"Can't you do nothing with her?" Christopher's solicitude was a sneer.

When Felicia arrived in the kitchen she had to complain that the pram was in the way.

"How do you expect me to sit down with that thing in the way?"

Christopher would reply that he didn't mind leaving the bloody thing out all night, and he would begin to bang it into the yard until Felicia gave further directions.

This subsidiary quarrel usually made it impossible for Felicia to still the child. She would look at the little screwed-up face with tenderness which was a snub for her husband. Christopher preferred not to look at the child lest his heart should be touched. He could hear her screaming without pity. So he would spread a newspaper on the table and pretend to read it.

"You and your newspaper," Felicia would say. "It's all you think of."

Christopher had been playing for this. He now had an excuse for indignation.

"I don't have to clean that bloody pram!" he would say. "I don't care what it looks like."

Felicia would enter upon a passion which made all her efforts with Sue unavailing. She hugged the child too hard and rocked it with too much violence. It raised its voice for a further prolonged scream.

At this point Christopher Homm knew that he could go out. He would put on his jacket that hung behind the kitchen door and step out into the street. Felicia was left with the child and a bitterness. He made his way to among the lights till he came to a little public house where men spoke little and in soft voices. The barman would pull him a pint of mild.

When he got back again the house would be quiet. Felicia would be getting ready for the morning. Christopher would nag her till she left off and went upstairs, where he would eat her coldly in a deliberate bed.

XXI

THE HOUSE FROM WHICH CHRISTOPHER HOMM BROKE
out into the new freedom of matrimony was dark, as the
street outside was dark. The blinds of the front room were
not always drawn, but dusty curtains obscured the lace-
covered furniture from those who passed on the pavement.
The piano could not sing into the street and the aspidistra
could neither choke nor breathe. Going in at the front door
one passed that shrouded room and was conscious of it as of
a corpse in the house. One came to the kitchen with the dark
red table-cloth and it was only then that a little light was
allowed to enter. This cavern was the haunt of Mother and
Dad, who there brooded over their children present and
absent, and it was from under these rocks that Christopher
had to escape when he went courting Felicia.

Mother and Dad became very heavy when it first became
apparent what Christopher was up to. Watching one another
like crabs across the fireplace, they had long claw-like conversations about what was afoot. Mother had white hair
already and the firm red face she had had always, and her
bones were long and still straight. The sentences she jabbed
out on to the hearthrug were propelled by a resentful grief.

"Chris doesn't need to go out after that girl like that.
There's time enough for that later on.

"It's not as if he was giving me a lot every week while he
is here. I thought I'd have him to help out for a year or two.

"But there you are, first one goes off and then the other.
All they think of is getting their own way."

Dad did not have to listen to these comments because he
had his own reasons for a sympathetic grief. Some burning

rheumatism had vaulted his shoulders, and his agonized bones pulled and stretched the strips of once powerful muscle that covered them. He spoke little for he was going to death without comfort and in a house where no one could speak to him. His family did not understand the world he had carried in him from his youth. Except for infrequent oracles that no one listened to, and the merest grunts and indications needed to propel him through the cycle of waking and eating, he had almost discarded speech. But he could maintain a conversation with Mother by parrying her jabs so that she had to go on if she were ever to kill him with her own grief.

To Mother's remarks about Christopher's courtship he would summon the consciousness to reply:

"He'll find out what he's in for soon enough."

That alone would give the conversation another ten minutes of slow broiling life because it was so much merely a defence of Dad's own sorrows that Mother had to find a way of discharging her grief over or through this barrier. When she succeeded Dad had to find a few more monosyllables to protect himself with.

"He's got to learn.

"He doesn't know what work is and he doesn't know what life is."

There was no help for Mother: there was no help for Chris: and could not Dad be left to get on with his dying?

Yet even to Dad Christopher's courtship was of some use, as an exercise for morosity. When the boy came in from a walk with Felicia, Dad could overwhelm his inexperience with a ferocious silence. It came out of the corner of the room where Dad was sitting and entangled and terrified the son like an octopus. The confidence which Christopher's body had temporarily acquired in the ancestral aims of love crept away and left the eyes shifty or downcast and the limbs without certain concatenation. Christopher slouched around to find an occupation. He would even help his mother with the supper things in order to have justification for his movements.

When Dad and Mother had got him at table they would begin a more active sport. Just as he lifted his bread and margarine to his mouth Mother, holding the teapot, would say:

"You been out with that girl again?"

Christopher, who was none the less a grown man, would look at his plate and rush the bread and margarine to his mouth to show that he was not put out by the question.

"We've been out for a walk."

Mother received this with a sneer. The answer fulfilled her worst apprehensions, yet it was not true. Her son and that girl would have been up to something else.

Dad breathed out heavily through his nose and noisily supped at his cup of tea. It was not necessary for him to say anything. He knew all about these things. It was a triviality or an imbecility that his son was engaged on. That was what was to be expected. The world was like that, and his son was weak and a fool.

Mother liked to elicit a few details.

"Did you go over the common?"

Christopher was cornered but he would show fight by saying that it was all right up there. Them white flowers was out, he said, as if seeking to placate his mother with a bouquet.

But Mother knew what the common was for.

"Did you have a sit-down up there?"

"Only a minute like. It was a bit cold."

Dad blew into his tea and gargled with the remains of it. As he set down his cup his eyes and Mother's met with unusual frankness. She was saying I told you so, and he was saying these appetites are death but Chris must go to it.

Chris was not to go to it too easily, however. The other children had already left home and this was the last disruption that life promised. There had been five dependent and subordinate heads around the table. One by one they had grown brazen and emboldened, had thrust their way out of the kitchen and had not come back. As each had left, the parents had turned with more cynical concentration on those that remained. After the first had gone they had known that there was no help for them, and they felt the children to be nuisances, but they would not for those reasons let them go. They feared more than anything the silence that would leave them to face one another across the hearthrug, each listening for the death-watch beetle in the other. For Dad there was a partial consolation in that he had himself resolved to die, but the very resolution gave him a stillness that threatened to prolong his dying.

The time came when Felicia had to be brought into the family on friendly terms. A Sunday was chosen, for in the comparative unhurry and silence of that day she could be studied more relentlessly. Dad was wearing his best waistcoat and trousers, and had a clean shirt with sleeves very neatly rolled up. Mother had on her best shiny dress, and a smile of extreme sweetness which was calculated to deter any girl from becoming her daughter-in-law. Christopher was very conscious, as he opened the door, of the meanness of his home, but in the passage the obscurity was such that it might have hidden treasure. There had been some question of waking the dead and using the front room for this occasion. Dad and Mother clawed the topic bitterly between them over the hearth for some time. Mother was for using the front room, although it meant a lot of work, because her own house was to be as much under inspection as the person of her future daughter-in-law. Christopher hoped that she would win the argument, for he felt that among the sombre magnificence of the old crotchet work his family could just avoid disgrace. But Dad was on principle against using the room, the principle being, apparently, not to upset everything just because that girl was coming. Moreover, he judged that in giving consent he would have been obliging his wife, and he felt very strongly that that was a thing he should do infrequently.

Christopher therefore had to put his hand in the small of the terrified Felicia's back and to push her onwards in the darkness till they came to the kitchen door. He was just kissing her on the nape of the neck to encourage her when Mother opened the door to exhibit her shining dress and her smile at its very sweetest.

"Ah, there you are, dear. I was wondering when you'd be coming."

The tone was as if she wanted Felicia to know that she was only pretending that it was an accident that she had opened the door at that moment and that really she had watched her through the closed door and could watch her even through the most solid brickwork. The table was big enough to prevent any freedom of circulation in the room, and Mother managed to hold Felicia pinned against the wall just inside the door while she played her deleterious smile upon the girl and held her for exhibition to Dad who was smiling foolishly from the other side of the room. When he saw the good-looking, embarrassed girl standing on the edge of his ordinarily gloomy haunt he forgot his principles and put himself out to be gallant. He even fell forward over the leg of a chair in an attempt to advance upon her.

"Pleased to meet you, miss."

He smiled idiotically.

Mother was not going to stand for much of this.

"Do you want to go upstairs, dear?"

Felicia, it was evident, was to be taken off, screaming if she must, to sit on the lavatory and to discard some of her clothes on to a bed so that Mother could talk to her away from the men. Felicia tried to indicate that she did not need to go upstairs, and that she could hang her coat beside Christopher's on a peg in the passage. But Mother smiled a new smile, this time of excessive understanding. As the older woman she knew better what a girl would want to do than did the girl herself. She was not going to be deprived of the joy of dragging her victim into the very heart of the female mysteries. As they went she looked as if she were only waiting to be out of earshot of the men to propound questions such as no man could ever properly hear the answers to.

In the kitchen there was a pause until Dad was prepared to concede that a sort of normality had re-established itself. Then he said, as if he were not at all disturbed and yet with a relish that was not altogether pleasant to see:

"That's a nice girl you've got there. Got a nice face."

Christopher could not reply to this. The tone comported, besides the rare excitement of an old man, the suggestion that it was surprising that a fool like Christopher should have chosen so well. To agree with Dad would have been to concur in the latter's estimate of his son.

At length Mother and Felicia reappeared. They had evidently established a sort of intimacy. Mother had so far asserted her rights that there was no danger now that Felicia would respond too complacently to Dad's "pleased-to-meet-you-miss" nor turn too much for support to Christopher. For the course of this visit she was one of the women of the house and she was to regard the men as her enemies.

Tea was already laid, somewhat elaborately. They sat down and as the meal went on Christopher could not help noticing the superiority of Felicia's manners over Mother's and Dad's. Yet the two old people were both trying. Between the two women there was, indeed, an ugly competition which Felicia had not quite tact enough to be the loser in.

As soon as tea was over Mother again smiled directively at Felicia and this time indicated that the two would do the washing-up. They withdrew with the crockery into the scullery, and shut the door as old Mrs Homm never did on these occasions. Christopher sat miserably listening to the sounds of incomprehensible conversation that went on behind that door. The tone, which was all he could catch, was alarmingly pleasant, and Felicia came out looking as if she had enjoyed the talk.

"Your mum's all right, isn't she?" she said to Christopher afterwards as, escaped at last, the two were once more walking along the street and breathing the common air.

"What did you talk about?" Christopher asked. He was genuinely puzzled for he knew of no subject on which you could have a friendly conversation with Mother.

"Oh, nothing," replied Felicia.

"But you must 'ave said something, all that time out there. I heard you was talking but I couldn't make out what you was saying."

"Nosy, aren't you?" Felicia felt as secure now as a wedded wife and she had no intention of allowing Christopher into any arcana.

The two walked on and talked of other things and of nothing. Presently Felicia said:

"Your old Dad gives your mum a bit of a time, don't he?"

Christopher thought this impertinent.

"I don't know as he does," he said. Christopher was beginning to feel, what he had never felt before, a solidarity with his father against the conspiring world of women.

"Dad likes to be left alone," he said. He said it as if in his turn he were stating a principle designed to guide his own future course of life.

XXII

FELICIA WAS STANDING AT THE CORNER OF A STREET
when Christopher first set eyes on her. She was there without
formed intention, and her body as night fell was filled with a
dreaming hope. But if Christopher had ventured to speak to
her, which he was far from doing, she would have fled, for she
was not yet at the moment of destroying her hope by realizing
it. The street was sombre and without gardens, and the
straight low house-fronts had an elegance she did not care
for. The colour of all the scene was not grey but a soft
sulphur-brown. Along the street pawed and clopped an
enormous carthorse, its shaggy head and fetlocks protruding
out of the darkness. Christopher Homm felt as he was, a
slight and unnoticed youth, and he hurried past horse and
girl to his home in one of the straight-fronted houses.

It was on a less sombre afternoon, at the week-end, that
Christopher encountered Felicia again. This time she stood
under the plane-trees of a paved open space, beside a hut
used by corporation employees to store their shovels, and her
friend, who was dumpier and almost a little ugly, was
allowed to dally beside her to show off Felicia's beauty.
Christopher also had a friend with him, a red-faced youth
whose enterprise was necessary to Christopher if he was not
merely to watch passing girls but to cheek them as was proper.

The atmosphere of this encounter was that of a legitimate
social occasion. Felicia had no fear when she had her friend
near her, and Christopher knew that he could outface the
occasion as a mere second to the youth with the red face. It
was the latter who carried the talk over its critical moments.
He had begun:

168

"D'you ever go with boys?"

Christopher had been appalled at his daring and the dumpy girl laughed and scuffed one foot to and fro while the grave Felicia shook her dull fairish hair and blushed. It was she who wanted to go with a boy, but the red face of the youth was turned with cupidity to the dumpy girl, who had given him what he took to be a welcome.

"I bet thee dust."

This time the dumpy girl turned invitingly away, pretending that she knew what the youth wanted and was ashamed. Felicia did not even stir, and Christopher Homm was filled with the mere sight of her and was far from any power of speech.

Another evening the four met again in the same place.

"You're a bit slow," Christopher's friend had said to him. Somehow the other two disappeared and left Felicia and Christopher standing embarressedly side by side.

Christopher would never have spoken had he not felt at last that honour demanded it. His friend would later ask him how he had got on and what would he say?

"Which way you going now?" he asked Felicia.

Felicia was in doubt whether she should answer. At length she said:

"I'm going home of course, what do you think?"

Christopher left it at that. He could not go with her.

Yet somehow in a week he was walking up the wider streets towards the hospital with this girl of unbelievable charm. Her magic took away the few words he had, and they walked on silently for miles through shabby and dishevelled quarters that he hardly knew. He was thinking only, as he approached each secluded turning, how he might kiss her, but the greater the agony of his mind the less the courage of his lips and hands. He was the possessor of so insubstantial a body that his will simply could not move it. If he succeeded in walking, it was by a necessity that would not permit him not to keep up with the girl.

Felicia showed in the face of this deepening abysm of dullness a growing self-possession. As they turned up one lane divided by an old iron post and shadowed by a high brick wall Christopher could almost have found resolution to seize her waist had not Felicia at that moment begun to talk collectedly of the shop where she worked.

"He's a funny chap, Mr Frithy, the shopkeeper that is, and he gives me queer looks sometimes but I don't care as long as he pays me my money at the end of the week. But it's dull when no customers comes in, I don't like doing nothing."

Christopher was thwarted and jealous but suddenly they were near home and he had to leave her. How would she ever know what he had taken her out for?

The next sort of walk the two went for was different. Now both could look grave and both could talk. Christopher sought desperately in his squalid mind and history for something he could boast of.

"I've got some relations in the country like. There's ducks and you should see my auntie pick up handfuls of worms to give them."

Felicia saw nothing when he said this and began her counterpoint.

"Mr Frithy got me to do the window at Christmas and he says he will another time when he wants it to look special."

Christopher did not notice that he had not been heard and he continued:

"It's funny the way them ducks swallow up the worms. But they do lay."

He saw the pallid eggs lying in groups under the hedge.

Felicia replied: "The thing is I take a bit of trouble over the window but he just puts things in anyhow. You should see the dust on 'em when I took them out like."

Christopher looked sideways and he was near the glowing cheek of Felicia. It was nice to have somebody who was interested in what you said.

"Of course she got hens too," he went on, and seeing the green field flecked with them he supposed that Felicia too had that pleasure. This time the girl was so quick to show her understanding that she cut him short.

"Mr Frithy was watching me when I climbed out of the window and I had to pull my skirt down quick."

Felicia laughed at the provocation she had given, and at last Christopher heard what she was saying. His exultation was driven out by a morose fury that rose in him from obscure internal parts. This time when he seized Felicia's waist it was in defiance.

In this mood and in silence he continued with her till he brought her out into an open common. Here his heart leapt because he might get close to her body. She did not exist for him except as an empty frame.

Felicia by way of defiance resumed her talk about the shop.

"I never knew all the different kinds of cigarette there is when I went there. But it's mostly Woods."

As her talk went on she made empty little pouts and frowns, and even gesticulated a little in a way that threatened to dislodge Christopher's arm. Christopher saw that she was pretending to be a person. He was frustrated and kept at bay by her behaving as if she were taking part in some great social occasion. He had hardly ever spoken to anyone but those of his family and a few boys he had known at school. Felicia felt her advantage.

"Of course we always has a party at home at Christmas and he let me have some sweets for it. There was cigarettes too and you should have seen some of the boys at them."

Christopher affirmed that he did not think much of parties but that he supposed they was all right for girls.

Felicia counter-affirmed with emphasis that some boys liked them. The way she said it suggested that they were more sensible boys than he was.

"What they like some of them is that bit of mistletoe up by the gas."

She laughed and Christopher imagined her smothered in lascivious kisses. He became stormy and silent, then said:

"What about a sit down here?"

Felicia thought it was too cold for sitting about much. And wouldn't the grass be damp? They walked on till they came to a coppice where Christopher practically pulled her down. As they lay there he felt a body at all points different from his own, and this difference made him believe in a similarity of minds. But even in his embraces Felicia made general conversation.

"I got to go out to tea next Sunday to my cousins.

"If you get a half day Wednesday you can look at the other shops that close on Saturdays."

Christopher's body was studying Felicia with earnestness at all the points at which each could be sensible of the other. He had scarcely unbuttoned her mackintosh when she jumped up and they started to walk back home. But after that he felt he had rights on her.

The months that went by, then a year or two, were for Christopher determined progress towards a naked body. His movements and his speech were fumbling, but he was all this time proud of himself because he was driven by a purpose stronger than any he could have invented. He did not even have to be conscious of it; it grew surely and without difficulty among all the confusions of his ordinary mind.

Felicia all this while exercised her intelligence. When this young man came blindly round to her, waiting as if she were a city about to fall, she set a series of problems to amuse him.

"I believe you can be just as good if you don't go to chapel."

Somehow with their limited vocabularies they would manage to discourse on the subject for a couple of hours, with Christopher fully sensible of the impropriety of pressing his attack too hard in the course of such deliberations.

"I don't believe everything's true you read in the papers."

This theme had not the sanctity of the other, but both Felicia and Christopher found that points to illustrate it came more readily to hand, so it kept Christopher without more than a couple of kisses for two hours and a half.

"I think girls ought to be allowed to have just as good a time as boys."

Christopher seized on this subject when it was proposed for disputation because his subterranean purposes understood it more quickly than his mere wit could have done. But Felicia deflected him and showed that she meant only that it wasn't fair that girls should have to help with laying tables and washing up and boys be let off like her brothers.

Christopher and Felicia also went deliberately to see things, which was really against Christopher's conscience. He had eyes when he chose to raise them from the ground but the images that filled his mind were so many photographs involuntarily taken.

"What about going to see those destroyers down the docks?"

Christopher was pleased at any suggestion for an outing and off they went. The sailors winked at Felicia and helped her up and down the companionway as if Christopher had not been there.

"He was a nice fellow the one that showed us round."

"But he wouldn't be a sailor if he could get a job. That's how they get them."

Christopher and Felicia were even known to go and look, as if they were interested, at the old castle.

"I bet that's old," Felicia said, looking at it as if she were appreciating something.

Christopher Homm could not see that it mattered if it were old.

In these excursions the minds of Christopher and Felicia were supposed to grow together.

"You want to get to know a young man pretty carefully before you let him touch you." That had been the advice of Felicia's mother once she had reluctantly recognized that her daughter was walking out.

Christopher's father advised him to make sure that Felicia was a good housekeeper. Christopher forgot this advice at once as having no relevance to the purposes that possessed him.

When the two quarrelled it was supposed that the growing union of their minds had been temporarily upset. The quarrels were made up with unnecessary kisses and Felicia, who was then the philosopher, would reason about the causes.

"But we do get on better than we used to," she would say. "It's a question of getting to know each other better like."

In time there would not be any discordances. It seemed a reason for prolonging the courtship.

Christopher bore this philosophy with patience because, unless he was unlucky, such discourses could be made a prelude to fresh and more daring holds. As the two lay side by side, making it up, he would, if he had formed an opinion, have claimed that he was understanding Felicia better.

"We're closer like, now," she said. They were certainly that.

The further Christopher groped into the lonely world of sensuality the more he felt he had found a companion. The greater his deception, the greater his joy.

Meanwhile Felicia was bringing her own scheme of things to a conclusion. The walks she and Christopher made now included tours of the shops where household goods were sold. They even paused once, though only tentatively, in front of a jeweller's.

Even when Christopher had been brought for a whole thirty minutes before the window of a furniture shop he did not know that it was as a preparation for matrimony. But Felicia obviously judged the exposure sufficient, and for their next walk she put on the dress that buttoned down the front.

XXIII

THE MYSTERIES OF FELICIA DID NOT OPEN BEFORE
Christopher until he had searched for his love elsewhere.
His first love had been for knowledge, a frail precursor who
stumbled and was replaced by the more enduring Felicia.

It was because Christopher had an awkward body and a
distaste for violence that he could not join the youths hooting
and howling about the lamp-posts, but must creep sorrow-
fully into the quiet places of the city where knowledge was
to be found. One of these haunts was a long arcade in the
recesses of which he could feel that he was unseen. What
was displayed before the little shop-fronts concealed him
from the cruelty of boys, and the arches protected him from
the wrath of heaven. It was a tame and human light that
filtered through the roof windows. There was old junk to be
stared at, idols and the castors of iron bedsteads, which were
equally wonderful to eyes that desired with agony to be full.
Christopher did not so much concentrate on these articles
as evade the rest of the world. He would have desired to be
alone, but as this is impossible he hoped to share the world
only with one insensible thing.

Further down the arcade was the temple of a more dis-
cursive knowledge. Here on a trestle table the tuppeny books
were put out for sale. Christopher dared not lift his eyes to
the more magnificent volumes behind the window glass, but
even with lowered lids he saw sometimes their shining and
proud array. These books had a look of opulence and a
power of their own. They did not merely rest in the window.
They were as if in a suspension which was dependent on
their own activity. And in the centre of the window was a

folio open to exhibit a Jacobean luxury of decorations upon its title-page, and grave and muscular men and women in full and unperturbed nakedness. The volumes Christopher could touch were grimy rather than dusty. His fingers ran lightly over their spines as if he hoped that one or other of the books would jump out of its place and give him knowledge. The books remained still, however, and he had no certain motive for choosing one of them rather than another. One glittered with a tawdry embossed lettering; one had pictures on the back in red and blue; some had no backs at all. He picked out one that proved to have sums in it, and he put that back; then he took another, and found a few words about a girl being carried off by her lover, but the next page proved disappointing. The next dip brought him a diagram that pretended, he thought incredibly, to portray the reproductive organs of the human female. He was trying to make this out when the shopkeeper came out, stood in the doorway, and looked at him.

Christopher was terrified at being caught in what was undoubtedly crime. He did not move at once, for that would have been to confess his fault, but after a moment turned the page to show only lines of indistinguishable type. The shopkeeper, as if to show that he knew that ruse, raised his arm quickly to scratch his head. Christopher slid the book back into its place.

To show the catholicity of his interests Christopher Homm began to take another book from its place. His eyes as he did so were so furtive, in their attempt to keep a watch at once on the book and the shopkeeper, that the latter made another and more disturbing move. He seized two books and slammed them together to get the dust out. Then he turned his round face once more on Christopher Homm and pushed out moist lips under his brown moustache. When he spoke it was as if he had for a long time inclined to the opinion he now conveyed but had been unwilling to express it until he had weighed everything with more than the necessary care.

"You'd better clear off," he said. "You're not the sort that buys books. You're the sort that pinches them though."

Christopher Homm had no answer to this insult. He was sent back with flaming cheeks to the world outside the arcade. He made a long détour, through the most public and crowded streets, to avoid the eyes of youths who might think him not sufficiently disreputable, and so reached home, where he re-read the newspaper that he had perused before setting out.

Another refuge, less often sought because it was more remote, was the exhibition of stuffed animals which passed as a museum of natural history. It was the more unnatural parts of the collection which appealed particularly to Christopher Homm. The stuffed deer and antelopes standing in the entrance hall looked shabby and merely human, and the giraffe was too high to be seen by Christopher's downcast eyes except when he was skirting the gallery and saw the beast's head appearing improbably on a level with his own boots. Christopher did not so much look at the exhibits as retreat occasionally from one caught sight of out of the corner of his eye. In the ecclesiastical silence of the museum he felt safe and he had therefore not, out of a desperate fear, to concentrate on any particular object. He had merely to avoid the more nefarious spirits or omens which must present themselves even there. Thus he steered under the vast bones of the whale, and beside the shining jaws of the alligator, into the emptier silence in the middle of the hall. One object, however, drew him by its own magical qualities. This was the trophy of some head-hunter that had found its way into a glass case next to the stuffed monkeys. To this dried and wrinkled head, to its very deadness and grotesqueness, Christopher Homm felt a kinship. He could stand before this as if he were talking to his alter ego. The head never spoke to him, however, and the nearest Christopher Homm got to friendship was to carry the image away with him so that at night he dreamed of his own shrunken head standing in the case beside that of the South Sea Islander.

This was too absurd a recollection for Christopher Homm to allow himself to carry into his waking life. But sometimes, when he walked about the streets, he imagined his own frightened head to have the qualities of that physical ghost. It was what it felt like to be looked at. If Christopher Homm desired to contemplate and know, it was only because by the exercise of this attention he could become unconscious of himself.

It was not often that the objects he encountered in the streets were able to give him that security. Only a most vivid impression which could hardly endure, could make him into a being that was seeing rather than seen. He would therefore take refuge from the streets in his own home. He would climb the dark stairs and lie at length on his bed with a paper. But what he saw there was scarcely more objective than spots floating before his eyes. The print crawled over his mind and he wanted to scratch. Some journals his mother bought were even more absorbing. If he brought one of these to his hide-out above stairs he could lose himself in a story that stirred uncomprehended emotions. He ignored the young men, stouter and more handsome than himself, who in the picture smiled over their square jaws and bunches of roses. His eyes like theirs were all for the shy and distracting girl in discreet clothes who lowered her lids before them. In the stories lust was always whetted by almost unbearable deprivation. The young man would go away, called by duty or merely too noble to speak. The girl would be entangled in the woes of a threatening blindness or sickness which in the end did not engulf her, or would coyly pretend devotion to a dying relative to coax her lover on. Christopher would be impelled to dream on, in a dream without definition, of situations that brought him close to some scene of youthful déshabille. In his dim mind he hardly knew whether or not there was a warm young body beside his in the darkness. Then a shout from downstairs, or a mere movement of self-disgust, would call him back to look at the narrow window through which came the destroying light. He looked out on derelict roof-tops and toppling chimney-pots, and his body boiled too restlesly for him to regard them as a calm world that could impart equanimity if it were looked at steadily enough.

Despairing of that outer world as of the inner world of reverie, he stood before the mirror and looked at his own extraordinary face. He could not do so without either twisting his mouth into a grimace or giving his eyes a look like a madman's. He could not contemplate either of these distorted images for long. He had to get his fingers to work. The mirror showed them crawling up his face before his will had directed them. Then he would peer more closely to find a pimple or a blackhead. He would squeeze it, and when he did so with effect he felt a satisfaction no larger than the part in question. He was ridding himself of little black or yellow atoms of his corruption. In his hunt he would press until his pale face was pink and blotchy.

Another shout from downstairs would generally take him away from this study and purification, but sometimes when there was no-one in the house or when it was bed-time he would take off his clothes in two or three movements and stand naked before the mirror. It was a pale thin body he saw, and he would throw back his head and shoulders and pull in his abdomen in the hope that with these improvements he would be handsome. It was, however, less beauty that he sought in himself than lineaments that would convince him of his own humanity. With stealth he would take from one of the drawers a treasure he had found in a dirty junk shop and had bought for sixpence. It was a cardboard model, about eighteen inches high, of a man's body, devised out of several thicknesses so that one could take off, first the outer skin to reveal the muscle, next the muscles to reveal the veins and arteries, and then that layer to reveal the various internal organs. Christopher Homm had concluded that this was the reality of man. He first compared his outer case with that of the model. In place of the latter's glowing pink he had only a sunless pallor. He observed on himself certain puny hairs not shown in the diagram. He knew that in comparison with what older men could show they were but the weakest of weeds. Then he turned over the first page of the model and tried to follow on his own figure the structure of the muscles. It was easier to see the structure of the bones. Where over the arms and chest of the model there were shown bulging red concatenations Christopher Homm could see only an unplumped skin. He could make some trace of reality appear in himself only by bending his arms with deliberate effort. By no contortion would anything appear that corresponded with the model's orderly array of abdominal muscles. The legs, however, strengthened by much walking about the streets, could easily be given something like the correct appearance. The next page presented less difficulty, for certain veins already protruded on Christopher's arms and legs, filled with a blue rotten blood moving slowly back to poison the heart.

But what of the inner parts? At this point Christopher left the mirror and went to lie on his bed and pound his abdomen in search of liver, stomach, and intestines. He might have them all, but were they the shape they should be? Sometimes he imagined that he was nothing but a bag of intestines; at other times he was convinced that his liver had swollen till it filled the whole lower part of his trunk. And what of his sexual organs? On this point his textbook was defective. On the first page the groin was covered by a huge emblem, half shield and half fig-leaf, which was labelled by an arrow from the margin "Genital Area." From the pages below there had been an excision. Christopher Homm was left morosely wondering whether what he had corresponded with any precision to the image that someone had carried off before the book came into his possession.

XXIV

SCHOOL FOR CHRISTOPHER HOMM HAD BEEN A PLACE of fear and cruelty. He would lie at home on the hearthrug on Sunday evening aching with the horror of what lay before him on the following morning. When the morning came he would stumble out into the street, always afraid to be late, and hurry between the watching houses until he came to the high wall of the school. The boys standing by the gate were there to torment him. As he went in the narrow way one might flick at him with a belt or a knotted rope, or another punch him in the stomach or make a grab at his fly-buttons. He did not resist, less because he was afraid than because his mind was so passive that he did not believe resistance to be possible. He had the overwhelming duty of getting inside the gate and he must pass the snarling dogs at the entrance. The gestures they made were the merest passes but he dreaded them as the initial horror of school. When he arrived in the asphalt playground he would avoid the wrestling scrums and the games of football and skirt the yard till he reached the shed where a few of the larger and more peaceful boys were playing at marbles or exchanging cigarette cards. His clothes were no worse than theirs but they seemed ill-fitting. He shrugged first one shoulder and then another as if that would make them settle down properly. Sometimes a meteor of boys would crash into him and send him sprawling on the ground. Once on his face he would look patiently at the mottling of the asphalt till he felt that the weight on top of him had been relieved. He stood up and it was a relief when the master came out and blew a whistle, even though that meant that the real horror of the day had begun.

At the first whistle all the boys were to stand still. Often one or two did not and the master shouted at them. At the second whistle everyone had to move quickly to his appointed place in the lines. There was a double line for each standard, and they were arranged with the smaller boys in front, immediately facing the master, and the bigger boys behind. If anyone talked in the lines the master shouted again. Sometimes he prowled behind and gave a boy a punch in the kidneys.

The files marched in one after the other and lined up in the assembly hall. The headmaster stood on the dais ready to see them come in. He was a short fat man with silver hair and he stood with his legs apart and his hands in his waistcoat pockets, and he eyed the boys as they came in with a contemptuous stare and a curl of his thick lips. Only when everyone was in place did he stir and it was to make some comment about the shuffling way the boys had marched, and to threaten to cane any offender who came in like that on the following day.

"And I don't mind how many of them there are."

The headmaster was bending himself to the day's work.

His next job was to pray. He ordered every boy to put his hands together and to close his eyes. He kept his own eyes open so that the boys should know that, whether or not God saw them, he did. Then he rapped out a prayer in a brutal and contemptuous voice. He gave out a hymn and the piano started to thump.

"When morning gilds the skies."

The words had nothing to do with the skies; they meant nothing to Christopher Homm except that, under the gloating eyes of the headmaster, he was to rejoin an eternity of threats and barbarisms. When the boys marched off to the class-rooms the late-comers were left in a single line before the headmaster. He would not accept any excuse, but he liked to listen to each in turn so that he could pretend to be merciful. Then he caned each boy and sent him off to the first lesson, which was scripture.

The young man who was Christopher's teacher sat at his tall desk swinging one leg free. He knew better than to believe in the extravagances of the Bible, but he would teach even that for a living. He looked out over the boys he was to drive it into.

"You don't know how lucky you are. In some countries instead of me there'd be a man with a horse-whip standing here."

Christopher Homm felt the whip lick over the heads of the class and knew gratitude. The young man swung his long cane to and fro as if he were wondering who to use it on.

A handbell sounded in the hall signifying the change from one alarm to another. The next lesson was arithmetic. The young man's muscles at once began to operate with a mechanical perfection.

"Long division in money!"

He gave a snarling laugh to think how many of the boys would be unable to do it. Christopher trembled. He was passing into a world where a series of precise obstacles would be put before him and he would have publicly to stumble. He dreaded to think what sneers and what penalties would be enacted. When the first boy was caned he averted his eyes.

The teacher was speaking rapidly and moving about the classroom with vigour. Manipulating these figures he felt the satisfaction he would have done in taking a machine to pieces. The universe was made of such stuff and he was master of it. He could see that everything in it fitted exactly.

He walked up and down the gangways cheerfully pulling ears and hair and banging exercise books on the desks.

Christopher felt him looking over his shoulder at the sums he had been fumbling with. He was pulled up by the ear.

"What's this?"

Christopher replied that these were his sums. He began to sit down again but the master roared.

"No stand up you great booby. All have a look at him!"

All the bones in Christopher's body felt a little out of alignment. He had no solid flesh to keep them in place.

"This is how that booby thinks you do long division in money!"

The master drew on the blackboard in exaggerated figures what Homm had written in his book.

"You fool!" he shouted.

He threw the book at Christopher's head and then turned without a word of explanation and cleaned the blackboard. The bell had rung again. He could go along to the staff room for a smoke.

For Christopher the bell meant ten minutes in the asphalt playground. He was left out of any games the boys organized. He hated this but he wanted to get away. If he played he would only show his incompetence.

When the break was over the morning parade was repeated.

"The headmaster is going to watch you march in and if there's anyone not *marching*, just walking, the headmaster wants to see him. You know what that means!"

When they got back to the classroom it was time for drawing.

"And I want to see something that looks real! I showed you perspective last time!"

While the boys were smudging their books there was a shout and a scream from the next classroom. A boy was thrown out into the corridor. Besides his scuffling feet there were footsteps of more than one master. In addition to the ordinary horror of punishment there was the unnatural horror of a boy resisting it.

The aroma of this disorder still hung about the school when the boys went home for dinner. A small child dressed in a man's jacket stiff with grease and coal-dust stood in the corridor with tear-stained cheeks and the eyes of a rat. He was shrivelled as small as his body would go and did not know whether he was allowed to move from that dark spot in the corridor.

Christopher Homm ran along the street to his home.

"Did you have a nice morning at school?" his mother asked.

Christopher replied that they had done arithmetic. It was a form of negative reply.

Mrs Homm had a notion that arithmetic would be useful, and it was a settled principle with her to pretend to her children that whatever was useful was pleasurable.

"I'm sure you'll have enjoyed that!"

She looked at her son with all the uncomprehending force of her firm red face. Christopher lowered his eyes and began to eat his dinner.

"Not too quickly now! You can't be in all that hurry to be back. I expect you want to be playing football with the boys in the yard."

Mrs Homm knew nothing of the habits of her son outside the house. Christopher's only anxiety was not to be one of the latecomers that, in the afternoon as in the morning, were lined up for the headmaster to cane.

As soon as he could he scuttled out of the house like a poisoned rat rushing off to find the water that would kill it. Reaching the gate of the school before the whistle had gone he had a release from anxiety that lasted just long enough to mark a new beginning the moment the master appeared.

It was a sultry afternoon and the master appropriated the menace of thunder. When the crash came it appeared to be the master who had released it. It was an unspeakable kindness when he said, as the rain began to fall, that the boys might trot into school without further formality.

Once inside the classroom, Christopher's own teacher took charge of the storm. The lights were put on, a strange thing at midday. Then the monitors had to close the windows.

"All scissors and metal articles to be put away."

It was supposed that they might attract the lightning. The master paced up and down in front of the class as if he were deciding which of the boys was to be struck. Then there was a further peal of thunder.

"Is it going to pass over, sir?"

It was not Christopher Homm who would have the temerity to ask such a question. But he looked up not unhappily as he apprehended that these great crashes were of a power even greater than that of the master.

It was as if this realization produced a relaxation. The master walked back across the front of the class like a human being or a cat. He began to tell stories.

"Once I knew someone who was struck by lightning. He was standing under a tree sheltering from the rain . . ."

The master was openly confessing that the storm was not his own.

The rest of the afternoon was passed in an almost general quiet and humility. Here and there a boy might use silly words in the hope of attracting attention, but there was much in the day that was mellow. No quiet could drive fear away, but the fear lay crushed at the bottom of Christopher's heart as it did on Sunday evenings when he was waiting for the weekly horror to begin. It was only in the face of impending action that the fear spread into all his limbs and buckled them.

The day was to close with a final action. In that action, however, he had no longer, as at school, to sit motionless while his nerves curled within him. It was a battle from which he could try to escape. When the bell went at last even he felt some relief. He had still to run the gauntlet but he could run it and go home.

Outside the school gate a small red-faced boy with screwed-up eyes and face was waiting for him. However hard Christopher ran out that boy and two or three of his fellow-torturers were waiting.

"Have you had the cane today?"

As he tried to get past they put their question in low, confidential voices, like a priest asking the name of a baby he was to baptise. Christopher was too much of a fool to lie or even to keep silent.

"If you haven't we're going to hurt you," said the red-faced boy. He imitated a master and added: "This is going to do you good."

Christopher Homm had then to go ahead on his homeward way with his eyes in the back of his head telling him that he was being maliciously followed. If he tried to hurry, the boys behind him hurried. If he crossed a road, they crossed too. He could not go out of his usual way. If he tried, he found that the boys were in front of him, wagging their heads like middle-aged men.

"No sonny, go the usual way. We couldn't do it to you this way."

He had to be driven into a narrow passage where they could bully him without being disturbed. As soon as he went between the high walls they were upon him. They dragged him, for greater secrecy, to where the passage went into an archway through a tall crumbling house. In this dark place they held him against the wall. The red-faced boy walked free and boasted of the pain he was going to inflict.

It was when some passer looked at the boys enquiringly that they loosened their hold and Christopher was free. As he turned to run off the red-faced boy threw a stone that raised a bump on Christopher's forehead, so that his father, saying goodnight to him from the corner chair, could say with a chuckle:

"I see you bin up to your larks again, Chris."

XXV

THE SCHOOL THAT TRAINED CHRISTOPHER HOMM'S mind was equally careful of his body. It was a fine animal that they had to begin with. A constipated, foul-breathed little boy with sallow skin drawn over bones that were no more than almost the right shape deserved whatever discouragement they could give him. The kindness of the masters was matched by the courage and spirit of the boy.

On the day of the week when the afternoon was given to what was called sport Christopher would, if the weather were at all doubtful, sit through the morning hoping with anxiety for a downpour. Whenever the weather brightened his heart sank; whenever rain began to fall his heart leapt to think that he might after all be left to cower all day at his desk and live unnoticed under the master's threats. Just before morning school broke up an emissary from the headmaster tapped at the door. He was going round to tell each teacher whether or not there was to be afternoon school.

"Please sir, the head says that sports is cancelled."

There was a groan from the class and Christopher had a sensation of reprieve.

But if the weather were fine the class would re-assemble that afternoon in the park to play football. It was an expanse of coarse grass with patches of brown where games had worn it bare. As Christopher trotted over it to reach his class's pitch he saw other sporting groups scattered far and wide. He felt like a soldier making his way over a desolate no-man's land. In the centre of any of the groups there might at any moment be heard the pong of a kicked football, and the dangerous missile would rise threateningly in the air. It was the boys who liked football kicking the ball about before they had to. Christopher hurried on to huddle with the inactive members of his own group until the moment when the whistle blew and he was given a place in a team.

One or two of the boys had football boots but most, including Christopher, played in their ordinary wear. Nobody changed for the game, but jackets were taken off and put in heaps on the ground to mark the goal-posts and the corners. One boy had a torn football jersey.

There were two games for the class. The teams for the first were picked by Christopher's red-faced enemy and another boy, both supreme footballers. As they chose their sides they put on the pompous look of fools at an office desk impressing their subordinates. They made the grimaces of people exercising judgment and even tact, but in fact they knew at the start exactly who they were going to try for. When the two full teams were picked Christopher was always amongst those left over.

The master shooed this remnant away to another pitch. When the first game had begun these had still not picked sides. At last the teacher, who was refereeing the first game, would interrupt it to stroll over and get the other one going. As there was no question, among these dregs, of finding a footballer, he picked the two biggest boys and told them to sort out teams. If the two sides turned out to be unequal Christopher was the man left over and the two captains tossed for him.

"Loser can 'ave 'n," said the boy who was spinning the coin.

The teacher went back to the real game and the boys in Christopher's lot began to kick the ball about. In this game there were fouls but no referee. That was a disadvantage. On the other hand, it was not necessary to become the victim of a foul if one got out of the way in time. Christopher generally managed to do this, and he would always have succeeded had the practice been to tackle only a player who had the ball. But some of the players, despairing of getting the ball, liked to kick a knee or an ankle for its own sake. Not that instruction on the rules and methods of the game was lacking. When the master paused from his exertion as referee of the first game he would bawl over to the second:

"Hey, keep moving there!"

The tempo of the game would increase for a few moments. Christopher in particular would run up and down the field keeping to the same latitude as the players and on the far side away from the teacher. In this way he hoped to give the impression that he was taking part in the game.

This pretence had to be differently conducted when, as happened from time to time, the master came to spend a few minutes with the second game. When he did this his first act was to stop it and count the players, to make sure that none of them had gone off early. If they were caught they said they were going to the lavatory, and Christopher had neither the boldness to escape nor the ingenuity to lie. When the teacher came he had consequently to play. The young man did not referee this game but joined in, first on one side and then on the other. Christopher ran up and down the field very fast. He would even tackle the master, who might have had the will to kick him but who also had prudence.

Christopher's body danced wearily up and down the pitch as long as the game lasted. He was like a marionette with the strings pulled at random. There was no sense in his spurts of energy nor in his subsidences. If he had had a mind it would not have moved with the body. It could not have done so for the body was without motive or reason. It was more like something hanging from a gallows than it was like inhabited flesh.

That flesh had to be exhibited in all its nudity and pallor

when, during the term called summer, the boys were each week exhorted to swim. To this festival of rhetoric and goose-flesh they were marched in two lines from school, their towels under their arms, as if it would not have been safe to give them any chance to escape. The master walked beside the class. Sometimes he was anxious not to be known as a warder and accordingly looked straight ahead or surveyed the houses they passed as if he were an insurance agent or a rent-collector. At other times he would shout like a drill-sergeant to prevent some indiscipline. On cold days he would taunt the boys sardonically with the iciness of the water they were soon to enter. He could do this because he was not the swimming instructor but remained on the side of the baths fully clothed.

The baths stood in the dusty park and were surrounded by high brick walls like a gaol. The top of the diving board could be seen over the top of the wall like the control towers from which escaping prisoners can be shot at. Before he had ever been inside the baths Christopher had seen maniacs hurling themselves or being hurled from this high scaffold, and then heard the splash and shouts that followed. He trembled to think that when he started to learn swimming he would himself be as remorselessly thrown down.

To his surprise the first lesson did not comport this extreme exercise. When the boys went through the turnstile Christopher Homm felt as if he were drowning. But he was left with consciousness enough to record what lay before him. An oblong of opaque green water, with a few dead leaves and cigarette ends as flotsam lapping the precipitous side. A dankness rose from it, and with this faint cold poison was mingled the smell of feet and armpits. It was this latter smell that prevailed when Christopher found himself in a cubicle with another boy. The doors were left open to the sky, to the tree-tops, and to the green death below. It was not a sexual shame that made Christopher hesitate to take off his shirt and trousers. He hated to expose to the compact, muscular boy beside him his own lean and almost rickety structure. When the whistle blew all the boys had to line up on the side of the bath. Christopher felt like a crow nailed to a barn door.

The swimming instructor was an old naval man in a sweater and white trousers. He introduced himself to the boys by walking along the rank and pinching the skinnier boys on the arm or shoulder with a

"You want a bit of muscle there, son!"

When he came to Christopher the instructor pinched him hard and looked incredulous.

"This one," he said, as if he were announcing the result of an experiment, "is made of matchsticks. He ought to float all right."

It was as if the bird on the barndoor had still some remnants of life in him. Christopher wriggled in grief.

When he had finished his inspection the instructor took up his station on the other side of the bath, so that he could take in the whole line at a glance and exercise his word of command. A ten-year-old fantasy took possession of him and he made the boys fall out and fall into line again several times before he began his exposition.

"Swimming," he said, standing to attention and addressing the small shivering men on the other side of the bath, "is the art of making progress through the water. It is a perfectly natural movement. If I was to throw any one of you boys into the deep end there's no doubt but you would swim."

In his anxiety Christopher hardly appreciated the form of construction which after all indicated a doubt in the mind of the instructor as to whether this were the best method of proceeding.

"This mode of making progress through the water is just like running."

Christopher felt a flicker in the nerves of his legs, but the instructor went on:

"You throw your arms forward so, straight out from the shoulder, then turn the 'ands round and continue them in a full sweep until they are level with the shoulder-blades. That will keep your 'ead up."

The row of boys was made to perform this exercise. As Christopher without vigour stretched out his arms to perform these movements he felt an absolute confidence that he would sink. You could not see what was at the bottom of the water.

"In a minute I'll 'ave you all jumping about in there like frogs."

It seemed as if the instructor would stand with arms crossed like an impassive devil while the damned burned in the icy lake below.

"Now for the leg movements. I hope you can all stand on one leg without falling in. I 'ad a boy 'ere nearly drowned hisself the other day."

While he was still on both his feet Christopher felt himself tottering. When he tried to balance on one leg and strike out with the other he fell back into the dressing cubicle.

"If you can't stay upright I'd just as soon you fell this way," said the instructor good-humouredly. With his flesh screwed up round his bones and all the muscles held stiff by cold and anxiety Christopher made futile attempts to carry out the proper movements.

When at last the moment came for the boys to take their frozen bodies into the water the instructor spoke as if he were giving a long-delayed permission.

"All right, you can get in now!"

Two boys who could swim dived in. Christopher thought they were lost, they disappeared so completely and for so long under the green sheet of water. But when they came up they splashed and jeered at those who were still on the side.

Each boy went in according to the vice of his nature. Some sat testing the water with their toes, and went in in the end not of their own volitions but of a force lent them by the taunts of others. Some leapt in not out of love but in the hope that they would be admired. Christopher Homm could not hope for admiration and he accepted taunts not as a challenge but as a just statement of his weakness. He had not even the distinction of being the last to go in. In the vast isolation he inhabited it needed finally no more than the barest flick of the mind to surrender his body to a necessity. He no longer even employed imagination to tell himself what element he was about to enter. He was seared with cold and the breath collapsed in his body. It was worse than he ever supposed possible.

"Put your head under!"

To that necessity too he bowed.

Such were the sports and pastimes of Christopher Homm's youth. Besides these social exercises, he would sometimes creep off alone carrying a jamjar, and lie on his stomach hoping for tiddlers at the edge of a soiled river. On the whole he preferred this. And indeed he resembled a fish more than he did a human being.

XXVI

CHRISTOPHER HOMM WAS BROUGHT UP IN A CHRISTIAN religion practised in a bethel or tabernacle embedded in the side of the sulphurous street where he lived. The frontage of this establishment was distinguished as being paler and blanker than that of the houses on either side of it. If their frontages and snug curtains suggested a soiled domesticity, the architecture of the bethel conveyed the full measure of man's emptiness. It was gothic in recollection of the ecclesiastical, and nineteenth-century committee room in recognition of the rights of the congregation to worship a god of their own election.

The right of election did not extend to minors. Every Sunday morning when Dad did not find something more interesting to do he insisted that the whole family should accompany him to the chapel. The children had to put on their tidy clothes, which were bought enormously big and not put into real use until they were on the point of becoming too small. Dad did not ask of the children anything he did not require of himself, and he got into his blue shiny suit which was too small already. The mornings when Mother could find something else to do were more numerous than the mornings when Dad could, and she was therefore sometimes brought along as a reluctant worshipper. But so that at any rate the congregation should not see that, she dressed as carefully as on the mornings when she came freely. The only difference in her appearance was the glowing frown under her veil when Dad had been inconsiderate. But her navy blue coat was as carefully brushed, the same glass eyes looked balefully from the fur about her shoulders and the same penetrating smell of moth-balls and eau-de-cologne hung about her.

This smell was the incense which Christopher Homm ever afterwards lacked at the places he worshipped at. It was faint as the family walked in procession along the street, Dad talking to Mother and answering no children's questions. When the bethel was reached and the family took its place in a pew the scent suddenly gathered force and it was indeed the very smell of the initial prayer, as the varnished yellow graining was the look of it.

The interior of the establishment was designed to accommodate two parties. In the pews on the ground were the Homms and femes who were to be addressed and edified. They were to be elevated, but never quite so high as those massed on the rostrum at the top end. The backcloth to the end was the organ; below, and facing the audience, was the choir, distinguished by their sheets of music and the fact that they whispered as a team. In front of them was the centre-piece, the bald head of the minister peeking over an enormous bible. Far away below him was the congregation and the table to which he would sometimes condescend.

The organ blasted and the bald head popped up to announce a hymn. The first verse was read out with declamatory passion:

> "*The people shout with might and main*
> *To make their holy meaning plain;*
> *Who wottest what that meaning is*
> *Shall lead them to eternal bliss.*"

When the hymn was over the first prayer began. This was the showpiece of the whole performance. The minister was speaking in a representative capacity, and he was careful that his points should go home to those on whom the renewal of his contract depended. The suspicion of gothic about the

199

building was matched by a suspicious archaism in the form of address which was combined, like the architecture, with matter more nearly contemporaneous.

"O Lord look Thou down on us here. We are not the servants of anyone on earth but of Thou who wast and art capable of throwing down the mightiest. We pray that Thou seest that we are not hindered by rich and wicked men who are also working against Thee. Thou art no doubt aware that there hath been dissatisfaction with the condition of some of our brethren toiling in great industries. Likewise Lord we pray for those men and women, many of them coloured, who are labouring under various oppressions from those same oppressors in the interests of a few. Open up thy treasures of wine and oil to all thy people O Lord."

The amen that responded to his final words showed that the speaker had hit the spirit of his audience. It might have done so less conclusively had not saying amen to the minister been the only form of participation, other than the singing of hymns, that was allowed to the congregation, so that if they were to express their zeal at all it must be by the heartiness of their assent.

Christopher Homm, wedged between his mother and the end of the pew, felt like a creature walking at the bottom of a great ocean of words. He looked through his hands during the prayer at the strained rhetorical face of the minister tossing about above him like some great ship on the surface. He watched the nape of the neck of the lady in front of him disappear under the rim of her hat and re-appear as she twitched and re-adjusted herself.

There was another hymn, and then the minister looked down on the audience with the smile of a salesman saying that here at last was something that was sure to appeal.

"Now this morning, instead of my reading the lesson, one of the little ones is going to say a piece out of the bible."

A little girl in white was launched by a group of women sitting in the front row and she began to mount the steps of the rostrum. Christopher felt for her in her difficult journey, but her prim ambitious face was not that of a child who needed sympathy.

She was not tall enough to look over the top of the bible. A titter of delight passed over the audience.

"There!

"Poor little thing!

"It's a shame!"

The minister jumped to his feet with the smile of a salesman who by now had sold it. He brought out a stool and picked up the child like a grocer taking out a box of his most expensive biscuits. The head and shoulders of the child appeared over the top of the bible.

In her excitement Mrs Homm thrust out her neck and slapped Christopher's knee because she was afraid that through inattention he would miss something.

The little girl looked straight ahead and began:

"THE BEATITUDES
Blessed are the poor in spirit; for theirs is the kingdom of heaven.
Blessed are they that mourn; for they shall be comforted.
Blessed are the meek: for they shall inherit the earth."

When this was finished the minister again shone his beams upon the audience and proceeded to give out the notices. For this he could adopt a merely fawning speech and a common language, but habit led him often to prefer to the ordinary word one which he hoped had a kind of biblical pomp.

"The Men's Bright Hour will gather in the afternoon at half past two, at half an hour after two o'clock. The speaker will be Councillor Swizz, who will speak about the challenge of bi-metallism.

"The Ladies' Monday Evening will meet tomorrow evening at seven thirty, when instead of the usual prayers there will be a discussion about ways and means of raising money at the forthcoming bazaar. This will be a special occasion and it is hoped that as many as possible of the ladies will be present.

"The Gags' Concert Party is giving a concert on Friday and I know some of the young people are determined that it shall be a rollicking show. You can get tickets from me or any of the sidesmen on leaving the chapel this morning. The price will be one shilling for adults and only sixpence for the kiddies.

"Hymn one hundred and seventy."

The announcement of the hymn meant that the notices were at an end.

> *"What I have sought and have not found*
> *Is love which surely doth abound."*

The minister preached a sermon that was a prolonged version of his prayer, with the difference that on this occasion he seemed less than before to be addressing himself to the congregation. When he had finished the congregation shook itself, and sang, and then dispersed with a distracted air as if during the speaker's monologue their attention had wandered irretrievably. The minister got to the door first and stood there bobbing his head up and down like a shopkeeper seeing his customers out of the shop.

"Why do they always play the organ when we are going out?" asked Christopher.

Mrs Homm sought to sweep away this question with a hysterical movement. She spoke in the sort of tone she might have adopted if one of her children had asked a rude question about a fellow-traveller in a tram.

"That's the voluntary," she said. Then she lifted her silly face and put a taut smile on it to show tolerance, indignation and a sense of all the implications of the question.

Christopher hated passing the minister at the door. He was so friendly. His great hand would be held out in greeting and Christopher would never take it until it was only an inch from his nose and his mother nudged him irritably with her knee. Dad passed by the minister like a pillar of cloud. A voice came out of him that was civil and even respectful, but so distant that the minister's antics had nothing to say to it. The minister tried to sober himself up to receive this handgrip, but always before he had steadied himself the cloud had passed.

The presence of the cloud at his back was Christopher's overmastering impression on leaving the bethel. Everything lightened when they were in the street. He and his sister could run home and the movement of the body produced a detension of the spirit. The cloud became smaller and there was a happy moment when Christopher and his sister were chattering and jumping at the front door. Then the cloud drew up to them, and mother started to instruct them as to how they were to stand, look, adjust their clothes, comb their hair again the moment they got in, and to emit a hundred other intrusivenesses.

Dad took out a bunch of keys to open the door. It was one of Mother's pieces of mock deference to allow him to do so on Sundays. For a moment his mind enlarged itself as if to comprehend an imaginary ownership. Then the family was all in the dark passage and they were like chemicals operating against one another to make an explosion.

"Sally lay the dinner!"

"Oh, ma!"

"You do and don't you complain every time I ask you to do anything."

"Dad would you chop up a few sticks. The chopper's just outside there."

"I can't go messing about with chopping now."

"I've got to do every blessed thing in this house!"

"What about Chris?"

"He'll chop his fingers off and then what?

"Well, you'll all want your dinners I suppose."

Then the doors opened and the party burst asunder. Mother went upstairs in a shaft of light; Dad went into the kitchen on his way to the backyard; Sally opened the door of the mausoleum merely because she would not go where work was.

Dad came back and moved about the house, made restless by hunger and his blue suit.

"When'll dinner be ready ma?"

"Why don't you take it off now?"

But Dad would neither go nor come. He could not even make up his mind to be oppressive. He pulled Sally's pigtails in the hope that that would be a joke and he even made overtures to Christopher as if he had just met him again after a long absence.

"Hullo, son, how are you getting on? All fine and perky this morning?"

Christopher receded bashfully into whatever part of the room seemed to offer most security. If dinner was still not ready his father followed him and nipped his biceps with finger and thumb.

"'Ow are these muscles getting along? You are a big strong chap you are and no mistake."

He chuckled in a puzzled and uneasy way. He could never understand why Christopher had not the muscles and vigour of the boys he remembered in his own village.

It was a relief to everybody when dinner was served.

"Now come and have it do while it's still hot!"

Mother would look pleadingly as she put the meat on the table. Dad would choose this moment to take off his jacket and roll up his sleeves.

When he had carved and Mother had served the vegetables everyone took a first mouthful in the one moment of
order that occurred throughout the meal. Mother chose this
moment to look brightly at Dad and make conversation.

"Did you think the minister preached a good sermon this
morning?"

Sometimes he would reply politely "Very good" and go on
eating. Sometimes he would pay attention, and when he did
he put down his knife and fork.

"They're all the same," he would say with deliberation,
"those windbags."

XXVII

IT WAS ONE WET SUMMER THAT CHRISTOPHER'S
parents arranged for him to spend a week with Auntie Janie.
The rain was dripping from the trees when he alighted from
the train. A high-necked figure in black was waiting for him
on the wooden platform. The train went on.

Christopher could not see Auntie Janie's house. There was
nothing but green dripping hedgerows, elm-trees ballooning
into a broken green sky, and the shining wet road.

"Here you are then, dear."

The voice of Auntie Janie was husky, kind and matter-of-fact.

"I suppose you're too big for a kiss."

She took his hand and they crossed the road to a lane
indicated by a white signpost.

"LONGHURST."

"It's only about a mile and a half along here," said
Auntie Janie. She released Christopher's hand and began to
walk with a brisk plodding step that Christopher found it hard
to keep up with.

"How's everybody at home?"

The voice was firm and husky still. Auntie Janie was
interested and hoped she wouldn't hear of any troubles, but
she didn't mind very much if she did.

"Quite well, thank you," said Christopher, remembering
what he had been told. "Mother sends her love."

It sounded silly, but he had discharged an obligation.

A girl on a bicycle came up in the opposite direction. She
stopped when she saw Auntie Janie and talked to her still
standing astride the frame. She spoke in the same low, husky
tones as the older woman.

"Good morning, Mrs Walker. I was wondering if I'd see you. I've just been over to Polly's with those chicks."

"She'll never do much with them," said Auntie Janie. The judgment was final but it comported neither scorn nor bitterness. Polly was like that.

"What are eggs fetching now in the shops?" asked the girl.

"I don't know," replied Aunt Janie. "I haven't been anywhere lately to see. I had to let Mrs Hammer have her dozen and leave her to settle up afterwards."

During this conversation Christopher kept within touching distance of his aunt's black skirt. The two women at least were human even if strangers, but the wet hedgerows with their fresh scents, and the cows grazing in the field on the other side of the gate, were too unfamiliar a world for Christopher to trust it.

"Who's the little boy?" The girl on the bicycle did not much want to know, but she looked at him in a kind, distracted sort of way, with the same indifference as she looked at the calves in the field opposite.

"This is Tom's boy," said Auntie Janie. "He's coming to see how we manage things out at Longhurst. Aren't you Chris?"

Christopher curled and smiled and was silent. He could not be afraid of their kindness but the unfamiliarity embarrassed him and he began already to feel sick for his yellow street.

The girl smiled and rode off and Auntie Janie and Christopher resumed their trudge through the lane.

"You tired Christopher?" asked Auntie Janie. "He's not used to using his legs."

Suddenly there were two or three houses to be seen and this was Longhurst. The lane branched leaving a small patch of common in the middle, and on the far side of that triangle stood a squat-towered church, with the churchyard separated from the common only by a ditch. The bell was tolling, so that the interval between each pong seemed very long, and the vicar in his surplice was waiting at the door to receive the dead. There was no sign of activity in any of the houses, till a woman appeared from a cottage on the left to peg her washing high above the cabbages in her garden.

"Who's that for, Jane?" she asked looking towards the church.

"That would be old Mrs Stone up at the Post Office."

"That's quickly then. She only died Thursday. I never heard about it until yesterday."

The woman hanging out the washing looked at Christopher's back as he and Aunt Janie made their way to a little stone house on the other fork of the road. Christopher felt her looking.

"Now whose boy'll that be I wonder?" She went indoors to consider the problem.

Auntie Janie's house was not elegant. It was one of a pair of semi-detached stone houses of squarish appearance, neither cottage nor villa. The hedges were not properly cut and there were weeds on the path and the pointed laths of the gate needed painting. But there were nasturtiums and a few well-cared for roses to give it colour, and in the bigger bed to the right of the house well-dressed rows of cabbages, lettuce, and onions, the whole backed by a flourishing row of runner beans.

"You come along in now," said Aunt Janie. She took the key from under the doormat and opened the door. The white and tabby cat sitting on the seat under the trellis arch surrounding the door opened one eye and tucked in its paws anew. Christopher saw Auntie's black back and skirt, the cat and the arch with its fading ramblers and felt an inexpressible grief. He did not even know that he was wishing that he was at home.

Auntie Janie showed to Christopher a plain little room with a single iron bedstead.

"That used to be Jim's room when he was at home. That's your soap and towel there." She showed him a little white-painted wash-stand. "The little house is out there in the garden if you want to do anything." It was a door covered with shabby maroon coloured paint at the end of a path through the cabbages.

Christopher was left to his own devices till dinner-time, and he did not wander beyond the low garden wall. The world outside was terribly open. If a heavy-booted farm worker or a woman with a basket came scuffing along the lane he retreated to the doorway, for you could not ignore people as you could in the street at home. They were slow and as large as life, and when they passed on the other side of the low wall they might have been in a room with you. They even called out "Hullo, son" as they passed. Christopher felt that this was a dangerous place.

At dinner time Aunt Janie popped her head out of the door and said:

"Come and have your dinner, Chris."

On a large white plate before him were three naked potatoes and two slices of cold lamb.

"I didn't put any beetroot on because I didn't know whether you'd like it." Christopher did not know what it was, but in a moment he found his plate made vivid by slices of purple flooded in a luminous juice. He tasted it gingerly and managed to eat some of it.

"You haven't got a very big appetite."

After dinner Aunt Janie went to lie down for a bit. The summer peace was eerie. Christopher went up to his room and stared out of the window. The common looked to him like a scene where some portentous event was about to happen. He flung himself on his bed and began to cry.

He lay there between sleep and weeping till late in the afternoon Auntie Janie called him down to feed the ducks. She had been working in the garden and had thrown into a tin the worms that now lay there twisting and interweaving. When Christopher appeared she led the way through a little gate in the hedge at the back of the garden. Christopher saw the rough wet grass of the paddock and the ducks making their way towards Aunt Janie and their food. White hens raced up from another corner of the field and Auntie Janie hurried to give the worms to her favourites before they arrived.

"They love them." She picked up a handful of the wriggling delicacies and threw them among the ducks, before whom they disappeared almost immediately.

"Would you like to give them the rest?" Auntie Jane held out the tin but Christopher shrank away. He was not afraid of the worms but the action of handling them seemed to be strange and unnatural. Auntie Jane turned up the tin quickly but one or two were lost to the hens.

"Ted's coming round after tea to kill a couple of those hens. Would you like to watch?"

Aunt Janie was busy now with her eyes. She and Christopher were walking round the edge of the paddock and looking for eggs in the long grass under the hedge.

"There's some lays just over there sometimes," she said. "You've got sharp young eyes, just see if you can see any."

Christopher found a luminous pale brown thing in the grass and handed it to Auntie Jane but he was still thinking of the killings that she proposed he should watch, and which she seemed now to have forgotten.

When they had had tea Auntie Jane said:

"You won't want to follow an old woman around all the time. There's boys out there on the green playing cricket. You can go with them. Most boys like a game of cricket, I know."

Christopher saw that here he had still to face all the old horrors of school as well as the strangeness that filled him with apprehension. He looked out of the window. There were indeed half a dozen boys at the game of cricket. The sickening crack of the ball on the bat evoked a world of fear.

Auntie Janie gave Christopher a puzzled look.

"You're a funny boy!" she said. Although Christopher winced he could feel that her low voice was not condemning him. She was willing to accept any sort of a boy, but she did not know yet what sort she had to do with. She was relieved when Christopher used this moment of doubt to remind her:

"You said summat about killing birds."

Auntie Janie again seemed to be taken a little by surprise.

"Oh, ah, you go down there to the shed you'll see him."

He was not to be eased into the strange scene by Auntie Janie. He had to go down the garden path, past the little house to the shed where tools and potatoes were stored and bunches of shallots were hung up to dry. When he peeped in he saw first the leggings of a young man who was doing something in front of an old carpenter's bench. When he had a full view he saw that he was pulling feathers from a bird under his arm. It was a white hen like the ones in the paddock. He worked deftly, with his features at perfect rest, and without any symptom of revulsion from the white flesh he brought to light or the limp strangled head. Christopher too felt no revulsion. He watched only in amazement. There was a calm about the whole scene that made it seem hopelessly remote from his anxious mind. He crept away without letting Ted see him.

It was when Christopher went to his bedroom that his full anxiety took possession of him. He looked out of the window and saw a man and a great carthorse in a distant field. Then again he fell upon his bed and tried not to weep.

Here he was, far away in the country, in an almost empty world, whose sides were so far from him that they seemed hardly to contain him. The people he saw, even Auntie Janie, were menacing, not with a personal malice but because of their patience and indifference. They expected him to be an animal nosing his way through the world. Auntie Janie's voice was tolerant, but she assumed that he was a separate creature with disposition of his own. How could he pass a week in this loneliness? He hit the pillow and then knocked his head against the iron bed-rails, hoping in this way to reach out to the frontiers of his sensibility.

XXVIII

CHRISTOPHER HOMM HAD UNDERGONE A TERRIBLE anxiety when he first approached the Infant's School. His mother took him by the hand, with the firm grip that meant coercion rather than protection, to see the head-mistress. The head-mistress was sitting on a dais in an empty hall. The visitor's footsteps rang as they walked through it towards her. It was an unsupported space, and Christopher's body shrank in fear. On one side he saw glass doors and windows behind which children crouched at their desks before erratic mistresses. The way to the woman on the dais was long and dusty, and when they arrived it was necessary to climb in order to have any effective speech with her. As Christopher stood by his mother he was on the wrong side of the desk to see the head-mistress, but he heard her soft, muddled voice.

"Oh, he certainly ought to come now. It's not really the time but if he's really that age we must fit him in some-how."

Christopher had hoped that admission might be refused, but he understood by what the head-mistress now said that it would not be. Suddenly she rose half out of her chair and Christopher saw her flabby face, at once irritable and kindly, bobbing at him over the top of the desk. She was only ascertaining that there was really a child there.

"When shall I send him?" asked Mrs Homm.

"Better send him straight away tomorrow."

Christopher went away knowing that he had only a few hours before he would be thrown into the pit. All the way home he felt as if he were falling through emptiness.

He was put at the back of the class in an empty classroom and told he could look at the board. It was covered with chalk marks but he did not know what they meant. A cold draught blew under the desks to visit his bare legs. They ached rheumatically and he began to cough to distract himself.

"Where's the new boy or girl?"

A long fierce head looked in at the opening door. Christopher hoped that he would not be seen.

"Oh, you're the one."

The teacher had seen him, and she carried her bony frame towards him. She had steel spectacles and there was no escaping her.

"Come and sit in the class opposite for now."

She took him out of the classroom and across the corridor to another room where there were a dozen children, something less than a regular class and who did not fill all the desks. They were wriggling about with distracted attention until the teacher rapped on the desk with a ruler. Then they all stared at her with cowed eyes.

"Here's another little boy come to join you."

As he went up the gangway to take his place Christopher felt that he was walking towards a resistant crowd. They did not hate him but there was no movement of generosity and he was not received. When he sat down he was merely attaching himself to their edge.

The teacher walked to the blackboard and began to tap it with the ruler. She gesticulated, screamed and crowed, throwing her body about as if it were a thing the parts of which could not be made to fit. All her rage to force them did not succeed, and from time to time she came to a dead stop. Then she stared at the children with her ill-adjusted eyes, and began to shout again as if she could not bear silence.

"Now, read the letters round the class!"

Christopher did not know what that meant, but he felt a great dread. He was no longer to be left a passive watcher of the teacher's contortions. She was holding out the ruler towards him and she was going to attack him.

"Begin with the new boy."

Her thin lips drew apart and teeth hesitated for a moment between them. Then they returned to their place under the top jaw.

Christopher fixed his eye on a particular nail in the floor-boards. He tried to use all his strength on that concentration, hoping thereby to render any other action impossible.

The teacher flaunted towards him so that all the air about him trembled.

"Is he shy or stupid?"

She pulled all her limbs up and then let them all hang as they would, with only her neck craning and turning. Her lips were drawn out in a long sneer.

She tapped on Christopher's desk with her ruler. He began to cower, but thought at last that he must look up. Those odd eyes behind the oval spectacles were staring down at him. He thought the teacher was going to spit at him.

"He's stupid! Look at him, he's a little fool!"

She was growing angry.

"Answer me, will you?"

Christopher managed to answer:

"What miss?"

"Read what's on the board."

Christopher looked at it through a swimming haze.

"Don't tell me you don't know your letters at your age!"

Christopher could offer no defence. He did not know his letters. He knew nothing. He would never be able to answer any questions.

The teacher recoiled from him.

"We'll see about you," she said.

Later in the morning Christopher was taken out of the classroom and led to another inhabited by children smaller than himself. He felt safer with them but he was the centre of some incomprehensible disgrace. His shining body looked tall as he stood before the small children at their desks while the headmistress talked about him to the teacher of this class.

"It's no use putting him any higher," she said. "He can't read."

The little children looked with scorn at this drooping big boy. He was a monster because he had not the attainments of his age.

In this class the children were seated two in a desk, and Christopher was pleased to find himself by a soft-fleshed girl too passive to offer him anything but comfort. He did not speak to her but sat there in the radiation of her person. It was her voice he followed when the class chanted together, counting blue and red beads on a frame or naming letters held up for their inspection.

Sometimes the teacher paused from letters and numbers to teach a mystical distinction of the sexes. If there was a bad smell, or a patch of wet on the floor, she insisted that a little boy had done it. Next time it happened she would send home all the little boys in the class. They were dirty, corrupted creatures, while little girls were a bliss of pink ribbons. Christopher watched the intent faces of the children who followed the teacher's lips and like himself comprehended nothing.

The playground was a tremulous world. Its boundaries, the school wall and the green iron railings, seemed actually to shake as he looked at them from the centre of the asphalt. All around him small children rushed hither and thither. They were big girls too, who seemed to him slightly unwholesome as they walked up and down arm in arm in their black stockings and their pinafores, chattering and giggling. Sometimes they stopped to address a child in a patronizing imitation of grown-up oppression.

"Now you dirty little thing, take your fingers out of your mouth."

"You'll cop it when your ma finds out what you done to your pinny."

The most characteristic arcana of this puzzling hemisphere were the offices where the children went to do their business. The term was appropriate, for these were indeed the matters of greatest moment that they had to discharge, and the offices were, moreover, like any market-place the legitimate centre of all comings and goings and much usual conversation.

Christopher did not discover them at once. He wanted to do something and stood in the middle of the playground and almost began to cry.

"D'you want to go to the offices?"

Christopher did not know, but he let himself be led by the hand and shoved into the smelly entrance. Against a wall with a drain at the bottom small boys were cheerfully squirting little streams of water. Christopher joined them but was more conscious of the stench of urine than of what he was doing.

When he was relieved he turned round and saw the rows of wooden doors he had all this time heard banging. Small boys and girls were going in and out. He went into one of the cubicles and looked down the round hole at the slow flowing stream with its bits of dirty newspaper. Then a bell was ringing and the infants had to re-assemble in their classes. Two by two they lined up, and Christopher managed to snuggle into a blank space in the line next to the little girl he sat by in the classroom.

The little girl, who noticed nothing and was merely soft,

was only an almost tangible edge of the great unreality that surrounded Christopher. That unreality remained for him uninhabited until he encountered in the playground a slight fair child who had eyes and lips. When Christopher first saw her she was already looking at him, separated by only a couple of yards of that desolate asphalt. He had no ability to answer her steady look, but stood still glancing at her from time to time. Then the bell went and she was lost.

He hardly specified his loss but his dim mind was restless until he saw her again. This time she spoke to him.

"What's your name?"

An exchange of names was the utmost treasure the two attained until one day Christopher held her hand as the children were filing two by two back to the school. It was then that two big boys from the street where he lived saw him as they pushed their jeering faces through the railings of the playground.

"Chris after the girls I'll tell your ma!"

The long fierce teacher jerked her body over to the railings and told the boys she would report them. They were gone, but Christopher felt chilled and broken. It seemed to him that everyone turned and looked at him and if he could he would have turned round his eye-balls so that he could see only the contents of his own dark and degraded head.

He sat in stupor throughout the succeeding lessons, and he was glad to find himself alone on the road home. As he raced along under the grey sky he was not even filled with terror, but with a dried-up resolution to go on because he must. He galloped on pretending he had to tear the air apart with his arms before he could struggle through. On one side of the road was the high wall of the workhouse; on the other stretched the corporation's acres of the dead.

XXIX

CHRISTOPHER HOMM WAS EARLY DISTINGUISHED AS one who preferred thought to action. "He's a thoughtful little boy," they said of him, but it was only because of his physical ineptitude. When he climbed out of bed in the morning he would sit for many minutes on the mat beside it staring at the castors, at the fibres of the mat, or at the blue and red patterned linoleum beside it. His mind did not seek for reasons, nor divide one thing from another, and his way of thinking was only looking.

The unified world was hard for him to break up into disparate objects, and as it is only the mind that can encompass such destruction that can generally be recognized by another as having thought, it might be held to reflect great credit on Mr and Mrs Homm that they were able to give that name to their son's inactivity.

Christopher's body was, it must be admitted, visibly equipped with the machinery of thought. A head larger than is usually found necessary for that operation balanced uncertainly on top of a neck that was already scraggy. He had narrow shoulders, a curved spine and limbs that were soft and skinny, and when he moved a stranger would have been uncertain whether it was a foetus or an old man out for a walk.

He had large eyes, made of fine materials and lacking only the play and rapidity of adjustment that are the early shapes of intellection. His mouth hung open a little, as if there could not be too many entrances to a head whose powers of comprehension were so small.

Once it had been decided that Christopher was thoughtful,

it was soon decided that various stimuli were needed to shake him out of his thoughts or dreams. In the first place there was the voice. Mrs Homm was particularly loud and assiduous in the application of it, and this stimulus might have worked had it not been applied so frequently that it soon seemed to be no more than the patter of hailstones on the roof of Christopher's world. Then there were the bare, impatient toes of parents getting up; they prodded into his almost exposed ribs in the hope of putting a bit of life into him. There was the compact frame of an energetic sister, who was encouraged to fly at him waving her arms and legs to rouse his spirit. None of these stimuli had the effect intended, for they travelled for miles within his easily permeable mind without him feeling thereby obliged to engage in any form of movement. The machinery which should connect such stimuli with the muscles and move them was somewhat defective.

Slow though he was, there came a time when Christopher Homm began to engage in a little independent action. He elected those forms of action which were most like thought, that is to say such as had no consequences which anyone could regard as important. He would sit for hours pushing bits of paper between the floorboards of his bedroom. This exercise was a conviction that they would come out on the other side of the world; it was also the contradiction of that thought, because below his bedroom was surely part of the downstairs. He would also make little mud pies in the back-yard. But he did not do so in order to bring these productions to his mother and father and win a smile. He laboured solely and gravely to convince himself that he could carve separable bits out of the too integrated world.

At meal-times Christopher's empty frame was propped on a chair set at the kitchen table. The other frames that sat round it were not empty. There was Mrs Homm, bustling, intrusive, afraid that if there were quiet the world would not go on. There was Mr Homm, chewing over a morose disappointment the nature of which he never succeeded in defining. Opposite Christopher there was Sally, lively and gesticulating, made with neat firm limbs to show up the weakness and incertitude of Christopher's structure.

Sally had not only strength but virtue. She ate like a ravenous puppy whatever was put before her.

"She ought to have been a boy," Mr Homm would comment. It was one expression of his unhappiness. He knew that it was not a satisfactory remark, and that it explained nothing.

"Why can't you eat up your dinner like Sally? Why can't you eat up your dinner like Sally?"

Mrs Homm's remarks were actions rather than thoughts. The words were rudimentary movements towards forcing things down Christopher's throat rather than questions to which she wanted an answer.

Christopher lolled in his chair with his head on one side, his face white and agonized. At each proferred mouthful of his dinner of mashed potato and gravy his stomach began to grow hard and sick till he was more aware of it than he was of the food before his lips.

"Why won't you eat it? Sall does! Come on I shall lose patience with you."

Mrs Homm had lost her patience years ago, and could no longer see the world except in her own desires. She gave up the attempt to make Christopher eat his dinner.

"Perhaps he'll make up with the pudding," she said. "It's semolina."

Christopher had once made the mistake of eating a plateful of semolina. He did it in a moment of distraction, when he was watching a spider walk round the salt-cellar, but the feat was attributed to a hearty appetite he was supposed to harbour for that delicacy. If therefore he could be forgiven for not eating his first course – and that was difficult – the criminality of any failure to eat his semolina was a matter of evidence.

The whole of Christopher's future turned on semolina. That was Mrs Homm's unshakable conviction.

"If he won't have anything else he must have his semolina," she would say. "We know he will eat that if he's made to. It's a wonderful body-builder and it's a good job it is."

Mr Homm looked at the slight collection of bones and silently joined Mrs Homm in the resolution that round them a body should be built. He was content with this conviction about the end to be reached; he assumed that his wife must know the method. It was women who provided food. As a child, he had eaten what was put before him and he had grown strong.

"Eat up your semolina and grow a big strong boy."

He would sometimes reason so far of cause and effect, but in the face of Christopher's wriggling and pouting resistance he could only sit glumly and, when he had finished his own meal, shuffle off and leave Mrs Homm to a distracted struggle.

On Sundays after dinner Mr Homm would go to his armchair in the corner of the kitchen and go to sleep. The cries and prevarications of mother and son still sporting with the semolina would reach him in his dreams. As Mrs Homm at last got up to clear the table he would drowsily open his eyes.

"Did he eat it up in the end?"

His murmur was an act of conscience, and it was as if he were thereby helping to build up his son's body. If the answer to his question were yes, he would close his eyes again with a gratified smile. If the answer were no, he would still close his eyes, but with the different look of a man who has made an almost superhuman effort in a noble cause but has had to admit himself defeated.

These little plays of eyes and mouth were mere movements of the superficies which Mr Homm undertook in faint recognition of an obligation to share in his wife's irritabilities. In his heart, from which his body was mainly fed, Mr Homm believed only in growth. He had put in his acorn and expected that his son would be an oak.

When Mrs Homm had done the washing up she would take off her apron and come and sit in the chair on the other side of the fireplace. Her engine was still running and she looked about for something to do. Often Sally would come and sit on a stool at her feet and Mrs Homm would re-arrange her ribbons, help her with her embroidery, or pull her about in a survey preliminary to the making of some new frock.

Christopher would sit on the hearthrug as close as he could get to his father's chair. He liked the peace and silence that emanated from that quarter. When Mr Homm sat up and began to warm his hand at the fire, Christopher liked to climb into the chair and lodge in the narrow space between the back of the chair and the broad track of his father's back.

Yet even he was glad when the stupor of the afternoon was broken by Mrs Homm saying, in a voice that conveyed at once resentment at her servile station and a satisfaction that she was the only person in the house capable of performing a useful action:

"Well, I suppose you'll be wanting your tea."

Mr Homm knew better than to show more than a playful willingness to take tea if it were prepared for him. But at heart he was eager for he believed that, if a certain muzziness could be cleared from his enormous frame, he might be able to perform some skilful action or perhaps even to think. His huge earth might know a spring, and Christopher, curled behind his back, nibbled a tiny offshoot of this false hope.

Tea was laid with a determined chatter and an interchange of womanly directions between Mrs Homm and her daughter, who for the occasion put on forty years in a flash. When Mrs Homm and Sally were both out in the scullery Mr Homm sometimes found a thought. He would turn round and take Christopher on his knee.

"You and me," he would say, "is the men."

Christopher stirred uneasily at the heavy responsibility of being like his father, and having spoken his thought Mr Homm grew troubled with a deeper thought that he could not speak. The frail peaky little boy on his knee somehow did not give satisfaction. He began lovingly and doubtfully to pinch him here and there. The suspicion he had was that the boy ought to be made of some other material.

This suspicion somehow became a horror as the long Sunday evening wore on. Mrs Homm and Sally would go off to the chapel but Mr Homm, who had long ago loosened his collar stud and rolled up his sleeves, would not take part in such outings at that time of night. Evening was the time for truth and not for what he felt to be a social falsity. He shuddered when he thought that Mrs Homm would come back and tell him that that wheedling minister had preached a very good sermon.

He sat back in his big chair looking into the fire, and sometimes got up and climbed the stairs to where Christopher was supposed to be asleep. It was difficult in the half-darkness to tell whether he was or not. Mr Homm could only see that there was a light head on the pillow, and if he put down his hand he could feel that it was wet with tears. Mr Homm would go downstairs and stare into the fire again.

When Mrs Homm and Sally came home and Sally had been put to bed Mr and Mrs Homm would have their bit of bread and cheese by the fire. Then, after a silence, Mr Homm would summon the conclusion of all those cogitations with which he had passed the evening.

"Christopher is a funny boy. I can't understand him."

A son should be like his father and Mr Homm felt that his was not. But he had not the sophistication to deplore what he could not understand. Mrs Homm was better educated.

"He'll certainly 'ave to smarten himself up a bit when he goes to school. 'E's a big cry-baby and the other boys'll laugh at him."

"Well, I don't suppose we'll have no more of them."

Mr and Mrs Homm agreed not to make any more children like that one.

It was time for bed and they shook off the constipating sloth of the sabbath. Mrs Homm brought in a pair of boots from the scullery.

"There you are, Dad. Put them there ready."

Mr Homm looked with satisfaction at these emblems of his toil that would take him out of the house early in the morning.

"Did you patch my breeches?"

Mrs Homm could smile peacefully because she had done that the night before.

When Christopher awoke he heard his dad going heavily downstairs. He dozed, and an hour later, got up and looked out of the window to see him rattling up the street with his milk-cart.

XXX

IT WAS NOT UNTIL CHRISTOPHER WAS TEN MONTHS old that he was christened. For the first months of his life Mr and Mrs Homm were more anxious about the duration of his sickly form in the world than about its resurrection. For the next few months the time and place of the christening were intermittently discussed. It was an excellent subject for domestic discord. Friends at the chapel, wagging their heads up and down as they stood on the pavement after evening service, would say to Mrs Homm:

"I suppose you'll be bringing the baby along to be christened one of these days."

They looked out for Christopher and his retinue each Sunday morning, expecting to see his long white robe and the best clothes of the Homm family placed in the front row ready for the operation. They saw nothing of the kind, however, so they took his big sister Sally into a corner and said:

"And when is your baby brother going to be christened, lovey? It will be nice, won't it?"

Sally at first replied with a smile and silence, but one interrogator drew from her:

"Dad says it's got to be done at Gran's church."

All the women closed on the little girl and became soft and sweet with the triumphant scandal of what had been extracted:

"Oh, no, dear, you must have made a mistake, dear. Your Dad wouldn't say that."

"He did."

Sally was firm and indignant and her questioners were delighted.

226

While they talked over the portents with one another Mr and Mrs Homm were having it out.

"I think we'd better ask the minister if he can do it next Sunday."

Mr Homm, who had hitherto evaded a decision rather than opposed the one his wife was set upon, said:

"What about Longhurst?"

Mrs Homm in her reply touched upon every thought on this subject that she had turned over in her mind in the last few months, with the exception of the one thought that had dominated her. She did not ask what the people at the chapel would say if she did not bring Christopher there.

"Well, Dad, think of the long train-ride out there on a Sunday. Your mother could come here to see him one Tuesday, there is no need for all that."

None the less, it was for Longhurst that the family set out on the morning of Christopher's christening. The first train did not leave till midday. Everything was therefore as inconvenient as possible. Mrs Homm, who did not want to go, arranged breakfast and dinner at such times and intervals as to prove this inconvenience. Breakfast was even later than usual, and Mrs Homm was thus able to make a great fuss about clearing up and getting meals at the same time. Moreover, as breakfast was late, everyone ate with hearty appetite and no-one wanted an early dinner. This gave Mrs Homm an opportunity of complaining about the effort she had wasted in getting the meal, and the bad effect not eating it would have on Sally; and she suggested that such inconveniences were inseparable from baptism at Longhurst.

Mrs Homm was encouraged in her efforts to make difficulties by the comparative passivity of Mr Homm. It was not Mr Homm's ordinary habit to tolerate his wife's complaints, nor indeed any activity of hers that interfered with the expression of his own will. But although he expected from her the most absolute submission, he could on this occasion barely suppress a sort of gratitude that she should have permitted him to tell his mother that she could expect them all that Sunday.

Mrs Homm replied to this gratitude, the expression of which was admittedly so rudimentary as to appear more like a surly indifference, by inciting Sally to be as troublesome as possible. This she did by insisting that the child had her most elaborate clothes and hair-style, involving all the intricacies of sashes and ribbons, and then scolding her for every detail of her appearance and, once they were on the way to the station, stopping every few minutes to adjust something. It was not her intention that the party should miss the train, for she liked company and she knew that Gran would provide a good tea without Mrs Homm having to bother about it. She merely designed that they should arrive at the station in the hurry and panic she knew Mr Homm hated.

The Homms entering the train thus managed to spread about them an impressive degree of squalor. Even before they had mounted, their coming was audible to the passengers already in the compartment. Christopher screamed as if the purpose of the expedition were to put the devil into him. He had been thoroughly shaken by being held in Mrs Homm's arms while the latter ran for half a mile along the road, and now to comfort him she pulled her arms tight as a vice. She was shouting "There, there, there" ecstatically to the baby and intermittently scolding Sally for having apparently lost a hair-ribbon which was, however, soon afterwards found inside the collar of her coat. Before this happened, however, Sally herself had been induced to blubber and Mr Homm had thrown in, in a gruff but penetrating voice which he used when he was ashamed of his family:

"For God's sake shut up Sall or I'll clout you."

The rain which had been falling throughout the journey and had obscured the windows stopped just as they got out of the train. The air was damp and clean and burdened with the scent of wet hay. Mr Homm put his finger in his collar to let a little of the air blow on the sweaty skin of his neck. Mrs Homm wrapped Christopher a little tighter lest any of this healthful air should reach him, and she likewise enjoined Sally to button herself up. Longhurst was a place of great peril to the health.

The family moved into the road and started to walk down the turning indicated by the signpost. Christopher was the centre of it. It was as if it were a rehearsal for his funeral procession. Mr Homm carried him with majestic pace like a true mourner, and the lugubrious eyes of Mrs Homm were on him to make sure that no part of the corpse showed. Sally, who hated walking, looked as if distracted by grief.

When the party arrived at the triangle of green that was Longhurst, three or four women in Sunday coats and hats were already gathered round the gate of Gran's cottage. They bobbed and bustled as if they were enjoying themselves. A melancholy and agricultural figure of a man in a blue suit stood by them at the door. When the Homms drew near to the gate the women began to address one another:

"There they are.

"They've come then.

"Look, just coming along now.

"They haven't missed the train then.

"I thought they was late.

"It sometimes is.

"It's taken them quite a time to walk here."

The women descended on the party like a flight of birds. Mr Homm placed the bundle containing Christopher in his wife's arms so that she could take the praise for him and he converted himself into a second statue by the door.

The women who had flown to assess Christopher began a second bout of chatter.

"Dear little mite.

"Was he sick in the train? They sometimes are I know.

"Can I hold him?"

When Christopher's puny white face was revealed there was a new consternation.

"Isn't he sweet?

"How heavy is he?

"Who's he like now?"

Christopher dribbled a little miserable spittle on to one corner of his chin, and his mother removed it with her pocket handkerchief. Then she moved forward and the others gave her precedence. She was going to show the baby to Gran.

She passed the two loafers under the trellis and was shown into the parlour where Gran was sitting in a lace-backed armchair wearing a black dress and a small bonnet on her white hair. She got up to receive her daughter-in-law with "So you have come then." She then took the baby from its mother as if it had been presented for inspection.

"So this is little Christopher. Who's he like, now? Does he take after your side? I can't see much Homm in him."

But Gran accepted the little offering, whether or not he had not succeeded in resembling anybody.

"I suppose you'll want to change him before you go over to the church?"

Christopher was prepared for the greater purification by the lesser purification of having his thighs and quarters wiped, under the eyes of as many women as could get into the room, of their mustard-like covering. When he was freshly arrayed in fair white napkins his skirts were pulled down again and Gran looked at the clock.

The progress to the church was not funereal. If young Mrs

Homm looked, among her in-laws, urban and embarrassed, they none the less made something of her with their laughing and bustling. Even the men would have smiled a little had their stiff collars permitted that exercise, and they walked with tentative but not unwilling feet, touching the top of the grass stealthily before they felt for the ground. A christening was an enactment known to be joyous and for this joy the square-towered church was the proper authority as the little post office was for the sale of stamps.

When the christening was over the vicar shooed the party gently out of the church. His surplice flapped and he was busy as about a matter of business. The women began to release the chatter they had stored up during the interval of respect and holiness.

"Wasn't the baby sweet?

"You must call him Christopher now!

"Bless him, there's time enough for that.

"I thought he was going to baptise the vicar!

"Oh, he wouldn't do that.

"I don't know so much. You'd better 'ave a look at him when you get back."

Once the party was inside Gran's house the new Christian was put in a bedroom and the door shut on him.

"Isn't 'e going to 'ave a bit of his own christening cake?"

This was the very proposal young Mrs Homm had foreseen and had resolved in advance not to countenance.

"Well Gran's cake never did any of them no harm."

There was a feeling that Mrs Homm was making an obeisance to the idols of hygiene and right feeding. One or two of the women took up positions at such distance that by their whispers they could let her know what they were thinking while retaining the reputation they hoped they might have for being too delicate to say such things where they could be overheard.

"Anyone would think no-one had had a baby before her.

"'Tisn't as if it was her first, like.

"It's all very well to be careful within reason.

"It's not as if he looked so healthy for all her fussing.

"Poor little thing, he don't stand a chance."

These darts fixed themselves as was intended at various points in Mrs Homm's spine. She went on talking to Gran and saying how nice the cake was, while Gran nodded her head up and down with a mysterious smile which might have been acceptance of the compliment or approval of the disparagements which she too could overhear.

Mrs Homm thought she would like to get out.

"You can't go before the eight o'clock train," said Gran, nodding still more with satisfaction at the trap she had set for her daughter-in-law.

But Mrs Homm had briefed herself.

"We could still get the five fifteen."

"Oh, no, there wouldn't be time. It would be such a rush dear."

Gran suggested not so much a physical impossibility as a moral unsuitability.

Mrs Homm was very firm.

"No, we'd better go, it'll be his bedtime."

The backbiters who had been gossiping apart closed on Mrs Homm.

"What, you're not off, are you? You've only just come!"

"Surely it wouldn't hurt the baby to stay up a bit on his christening night?"

"Bless 'im, he'll sleep in the train, good as gold."

Mrs Homm ignored the mere miscellaneous cousins but she felt obliged to answer her mother-in-law.

"If he doesn't get a good night's sleep he's never the same next day."

"Of course you must do as you think best," said Gran. It was clear, however, that what Mrs Homm thought best was not the best.

This ambiguous compliance on the part of Gran was a sign for the other women to give way in a mocking circle. Mrs Homm found the way open for her as for a queen. But she had still to secure her king.

"Where's Tom gone to?" she asked.

It was a dialogue between Gran and Auntie Janie which answered this question.

"D'you know where Tom's gone to, Janie?"

"He'll have gone outside with some of the others."

"The men like to get together sometimes same as we do." Gran nodded to emphasize the pleasure Mrs Homm must feel at being with the Longhurst women.

Mrs Homm did not wait for a movement of sympathy but marched out of the room and up the stairs to rescue Christopher. He was lying awake looking at branches waving through the window.

Mrs Homm put on her own hat and coat and seized him and swathed him. As she went down the stairs she could see her husband being brought back captive from the garden. He was making no response to the suggestion that he should wait for a later train. He fell mutely in beside his wife, and Sally joined them without any criticism being made of her appearance.

"You must bring him back to see us when he's a bit older," said Gran. "He'll like the animals."

Mrs Homm clutched him tight and declined Mr Homm's offer to carry him. She marched off ahead of her family, leading like an intrepid explorer.

The new Christian was sick on the way home.

"I knew it wouldn't do him any good," wailed Mrs Homm.

XXXI

CHRISTOPHER HOMM HAD BEEN BORN IN THE BACK
bedroom of the house in which he spent his childhood. It
was autumn; the plane-trees from the square at the end of the
street sent a few dead leaves to play outside the door. Mr
Homm senior was awakened by a jab from his wife's knee.
As his consciousness opened upon the soiled bedroom with
the gas-lit moon looking through the curtains he felt the pang
of a man on whom terrible obligations rested. His wife was
now half sitting up in bed.

"Go and get Mrs Smart, dear. I can feel it's coming soon."

There was no anxiety about this request for Mrs Homm
had an indisputable right to make it. Mr Homm got out of
bed and at once assumed a formal gentleness.

"All right, dear. Don't you worry. Would you like a cup
of tea?"

He made this offer less out of kindness than because he
sought to delay the mission he was about to go on.

He thought of the many duties before him and hoped that
the case was not as urgent as all that. He put on his shirt and
trousers and when he was downstairs put his old mackintosh
over them. Then he made his way along the dank street. It
was that moment before dawn when it is uncertain whether
the streets are lit by the heavens or by the mere contrivances
of man. A cat crouching on the edge of the pavement elevated
itself as he passed till legs and tail were stretched to the
utmost perpendicularity.

Mr Homm could understand the cat's movement. He
expected that his appearance at that hour of the night should
cause astonishment and displeasure. The cat was merely

enacting the indignation he expected to find in Mrs Smart, who would undoubtedly think he ought to have waited till morning. Mr Homm was more conscious of the danger he was incurring than of the hazards that confronted his wife.

He turned the next street-corner under the lamp-post and crept past the flat-chested houses till he came to Mrs Smart's. It was by an action performed without his will that he knocked at the door.

Mrs Smart at last pulled up the bedroom window and looked down on him. With her arms stretched out to seize the window-sill she looked like some cloudy and rebellious orator.

"Who's there?"

Mr Homm asked in a loud voice if she could come along to Mrs Homm's now. From her darkened look he thought she was going to refuse. But Mrs Smart was punctilious in her trade and made no difficulties.

"Tell her I'll be along right away."

Mr Homm had hardly reported the interview to his wife when Mrs Smart bustled in. It was evident from her tone that from henceforward Mr Homm was to be ignored or to be used as a servant.

"How are you, dearie?" she asked, pushing past him. "Do you feel anything?"

Mrs Smart got her customer out of bed.

"Walk up and down dearie. It won't hurt you. Where's the things?"

Mrs Homm moved around the room and took clean sheets and pillow cases from the chest of drawers. Mrs Smart helped her to remake the bed.

"Your 'usband can take the dirty clothes downstairs."

Mr Homm, who did not like to be commanded, was none the less glad to escape. Once in the kitchen he began to fill the kettle and make preparations for tea.

"We shall want all the pots and pans you've got for hot water."

Mrs Smart had appeared and she drove Mr Homm and his plans into a corner. It looked as if he might never get his tea. He began to turn out the pots and pans and fill them with cold water. Then Mrs Smart noticed the kettle was boiling.

"We shan't want that water just yet," she said sharply. "I'll just make a cup of tea."

She did not want to be kind to Mr Homm but she ignored his competence in this matter. Moreover, she liked to put the tea in the pot herself. Mr Homm was astonished at the number of spoonfuls.

"You can take a cup up to your wife." Mrs Smart handed one over and settled down with her own cup. "I daresay there'll be one for you when you come down."

When he did Mrs Smart had settled herself in his arm-chair. She smiled impregnably and grew more squat. Was she not the goddess who was to preside over his son's birth? She looked as if she would as soon have strangled a child as nursed it.

"I want you to find me a bit of board and a yard or two of clothes-line."

There was no doubt that the woman was a murderer. Mr Homm looked at her in question.

"What sort of a bit of board?"

The impregnable smile of Mrs Smart grew more contemptuous.

"To make a wooden 'ead for your son."

Mr Homm went out to a shed at the back uncertain what was wanted. He found a bit of cord first and brought that back.

Mrs Smart was starting her second cup of tea.

"Give it here," she said. "That's no good."

She took the cord and pulled it to pieces as if it had been cotton.

"I want some strong stuff. Take down the clothes-line if you ain't got nothing else."

Mr Homm went into the yard and took down the clothes-line. As he stood before the totem-pole from which it was suspended, untying the knot, he seemed to be a man about strange devotions. While he was still in the position the first light fell on the house in which the victim was about to be led to his life.

Mrs Smart laid across her knee the board Mr Homm finally found, and she folded the clothes-line into neat lengths on top. Then she got up, tucking the board under one arm and swinging the coiled rope in the other as if she were going to whip somebody.

There was a prolonged moo from upstairs.

"That'll be your calf asking to be let out."

Mrs Smart went upstairs with her implements.

"I'll put this for your feet, dearie," she said, laying the board along the bottom of the bed and against the rail. "You can press on that, go on, hard."

Mrs Smart then tied a noose about the rail and put the other end of it within reach of her patient.

"Pull on that when you press down with your feet, like I told you when you had the little girl."

Mrs Homm lay sweating on the pillow, her hair tousled. The first pains were over, and she waited for the next. Mrs Smart assembled pans and buckets about the bed. She looked like a workman come to clean out a sewer.

The milk-cart rattled past under the window.

"Is it that time already?" asked Mrs Homm.

Mrs Smart sniffed and looked out of the window.

"'E don't generally come down 'ere till later do 'e?"

Mr Homm bent low over his horse like a charioteer.

"This'll be eleven I done this year. All round the district too."

"You wouldn't think there was so many," said Mrs Homm.

"Oh you would, dearie, if you was me. Go on pushing and pulling," she added, for she did not like to see her patient slacking. "There's always some on the way. It's nothing really. There was twins last week, over at Canvey Street, stuck together. They didn't live long. I seen some funny things. There was one that had his toes all stuck together in a club."

Mrs Homm groaned in a mere sickness of the flesh.

"That's not the right noise," said the midwife sharply. "Now let me hear you." She demonstrated fiercely what propitiatory sound should be made. "Try again!"

She sat on a chair beside the bed and looked with satisfaction at the woman writhing before her.

"I wonder if this is going to be a long one."

She did not seem to mind. Her eyes gleamed to look on this distress.

"There's somebody coming!"

She got up in fury and threw up the sash of the window. She could just see Mr Homm and the doctor entering the house at the door below.

"No-one told 'im to bring 'im!"

The doctor came upstairs two at a time and pushed his way into the room.

"What are you doing here?" he shouted at Mrs Smart. "I thought you'd done enough damage for one year!"

Mrs Smart was strong enough for the doctor.

"Don't you talk about doing damage," she said. "I could tell some tales."

The doctor pushed her away from the bed and began to examine the patient with an affectation of care.

"What's this contraption?" he asked. "You'll strangle somebody one day with your ropes. Here, give the patient your arm and let her hold on to that."

Mrs Smart held out her fore-arm for Mrs Homm to grip, but she turned flaming eyes on the doctor.

"You leave my contraption there as you call it. I've only got one pair of hands and I'll be needing them somewhere else in a minute."

"While I'm here I'm in charge," said the doctor. "You do as you're told."

The doctor lit a cigarette.

"It's not going to happen yet a-while," he said.

"Well, you won't find nothing to drink in this house."

The doctor looked as if he was going to hit Mrs Smart. But instead he turned and went out of the room. The little coward crouching inside the flesh and bed-clothes could hear him clumping downstairs.

Mr Homm stood in the passage below. He had his back to the wall, and was flattened as much as so powerful a man could be.

"Why didn't you tell me you had the midwife?"

"You know the trouble she had last time, doctor. I thought I ought to fetch you."

"You ought to have told me in the first place."

"Is it going to be all right, doctor?"

"How do I know whether it'll be all right with that woman there?"

The doctor went out and Mr Homm climbed the stairs. He tapped at the bedroom door and looked at his wife lying in pain on the bed.

Christopher crouched in his blindness. He was about to set out on the road to Torrington Street, and if he had known how bitter the journey was to be he would not have come.